The *Jonathan* leaves before nightfall. Will you be on it?"

"Alone?"

Simon smiled slightly. "Oh, you won't be alone. The London Company is sending out ninety maidens to become brides of the men in their Virginia colony. One more woman won't be noticed, and if you conceal your identity and mingle with the other women, no one should recognize you."

Hayley bowed her head in her hands, tendrils of auburn hair disrupted during her restless slumber tumbling over her shoulders. Did Simon realize what he was asking? She would leave home and family, uninformed of whether or not they would live or die, unprepared for what Virginia might hold.

All her life she'd depended on others and had been waited upon—making no decisions; doing no work. She'd been taught the duties of a queen, and had an education superior to any other woman of that time. But she had never before now had to use that education; now she was to be cast upon her own resources. No, not her own resources, alone. God was still her guide and protector through this troubled time. Encouraged by the thought, she lifted her head.

"I'll sail on the *Jonathan*."

Come Gentle Spring

Spring

Sequel to *Where Morning Dawns*

IRENE B. BRAND

Serenade/Saga
BOOKS

of the Zondervan Publishing House
Grand Rapids, Michigan

A Note from the Author:
I love to hear from my readers! You may correspond with me by writing:
    Irene Brand
    Author Relations
    1415 Lake Drive, S.E.
    Grand Rapids, Michigan 49506

COME GENTLE SPRING
Copyright © 1986 by Irene B. Brand

Serenade/Saga is an imprint of Zondervan Publishing House,
1415 Lake Drive, S.E., Grand Rapids, MI 49506.

ISBN 0-310-47661-5

Scripture quotations are taken from the King James Version of the Bible.

Edited by Nancye Willis
Designed by Kim Koning

Printed in the United States of America

86 87 88 89 90 91 / EE / 9 8 7 6 5 4 3 2 1

To my brothers and sisters

A NOTE TO THE READER

James I, in all probability, was the only child of Mary, Queen of Scots to live to maturity. A legend, however, suggests that Mary gave birth to a daughter in February 1568, and that child grew up as a nun in France. This supposition was addressed in the historical novel, *Unknown To History* by Charlotte M. Yonge. (See *Mary Queen of Scots,* by Antonia Fraser, Delacorte Press, 1969, New York, p. 344).

chapter

1

Spring 1620

AS LONG AS SHE COULD REMEMBER, Hayley had been groomed to become Queen of England. Now that the time had arrived, she looked forward to the event with neither anxiety nor anticipation.

Sitting beneath the portrait of her grandmother, Mary, Queen of Scots, Hayley's face was as serene and beautiful as that of her ancestor. In the soft candlelight, her auburn hair resembled burnished copper, and the dim light revealed green flecks in her amber eyes. The glowing profusion of hair, swept back from a high forehead over a fashionable wire headpiece, was adorned with glittering diamonds and rubies.

Her face formed a perfect oval, from which almond-shaped eyes gleamed as she compared her appearance to that of her famed kinswoman. Hayley's remarkable likeness to that of the ill-fated Scot queen was her family's hope—that which would make her England's ruler.

Suddenly the door burst open, and her father's brother, Simon Douglas, rushed into the room. He closed the door, quietly shoving a bolt into place. Striding toward the fireplace, Douglas touched a spot on the chimney, and a panel opened to reveal a small room, which he motioned imperiously for Hayley to enter. As she did so without comment, Douglas extinguished the candle and crowded in beside Hayley, and the closing door quickly plunged them into darkness.

Through the thin panel, Hayley heard pounding on the bedroom door, and her body tensed. No sound except her uncle's rapid breathing could she discern. He paused only a moment before he took Hayley's hand and guided her through the blackness, her shoulder often brushing the cold walls of the narrow hall through which they hurried.

Strange, Hayley thought. *I lived in this house seventeen years without realizing a secret passage led out of my own bedroom.* Or had the passage been added after she left the house eight years before?

"What happened?" she whispered, sensing her uncle's need for quiet.

"Steps," he muttered, and Hayley's feet groped gingerly into emptiness. Finally she lifted her long skirts, which were proving a hindrance to her movements on the deep steps, but being unable to hold on to the wall gave her a feeling of helplessness, so she dropped them again.

Mentally Hayley counted forty steps before reaching the bottom of the stairway. Then they walked for several minutes on level ground. From the dank, musty smell, Hayley decided they must be in the wine cellars. When Simon stopped suddenly, Hayley bumped into him. He released her hand, and she heard the sound of a door being cautiously opened. A momentary sliver of light beamed.

"Don't move," Simon commanded. "I'll return in a minute."

Again Hayley was plunged into darkness with the closing of the door. What could have happened to the rest of her family?

The door creaked, and Hayley drew a sharp breath until she recognized the squat figure of her uncle. He carried a small bundle in his hand, and she heard it drop to the floor with a thud when the door closed. A flash of light, and a short wall candle was ignited.

"If we hurry, I think we can still get away."

"But what about the others? Roger? Father? Robert?"

"I don't know," he said impatiently. "I was stationed at the top of the landing to take care of you if anything happened to change our plans. All had gone well, we thought, but before the last of our party arrived, the door was thrust open and about a dozen king's men burst into the hall. I ran to get you to safety." His brow furrowed with worry. "I don't know what happened," he repeated.

Hayley started toward the door. "Well, I'm going to find out. Are we in the cellars of father's house?"

Simon grabbed her arm, and his face was stern. "You'll do nothing of the kind. If you are captured our whole plot is ruined. You're the key to the success of this venture, and you're going to a place of safety."

Hayley tried to pull her arm free. "I want to know what has happened to Roger."

"Whatever has happened to Roger is too late for us to undo. Put on these clothes. We still have a chance to escape."

9

Simon handed Hayley a pair of linen breeches and a dirty doublet. Servants' clothes! Why did her uncle want her to wear them? Hayley wrinkled her nose at the unpleasant odor.

Turning his back on her, Simon stripped off his velvet doublet and breeches and replaced them with an outfit similar to the one he had thrust into Hayley's hands. Perhaps sensing that she was doing nothing, Simon demanded sternly, "Hayley, get into those clothes. Don't you realize your life is in danger, and every minute is important?"

"And don't you realize that never in my life have I changed my own clothes? This dress must have forty buttons up its back. My serving maid took almost an hour to dress me this afternoon."

Simon Douglas swung toward her. "We don't have time for buttons!" With one jerk of his arms, he split her velvet dress down the front, finally and surely convincing Hayley of their peril.

Turning away from her uncle, with awkward hands she removed her chemise and pantaloons and as quickly as possible, donned the ill-fitting, foul-smelling garments. She knelt on the cold floor to untie her silk slippers, which she replaced with heavy leather boots, much too large for her slender feet. Simon handed her a woolen cap, which she pulled tightly over her hair. In the morning the stable boy would no doubt wonder what had happened to his clothes.

Wadding her discarded garments into a ball, Simon stuffed them behind a loose stone in the wall. With a sweep of his hand, he extinguished the candle and moved cautiously toward the door.

Hayley hesitated before moving into London's dark, drippy night. March in London was always damp and miserable, and Hayley longed for the spring. When she had left Exeter in Devonshire a few days ago, she had seen some slight suggestion of the waning of winter, but here in mid-London, the new season seemed far away. Hayley stayed close behind Simon as he slid guardedly along the side of the building. Her eyes adjusted to the darkness, and the familiar buildings, located several streets away from her father's home, told Hayley they must have traveled underneath the street in the tunnel they had followed.

Simon halted his steps and walked beside her as they started down a wide street. Oil-soaked wood, burning in metal baskets on high poles, gave some light, but the dampness caused a hazy atmosphere. Hayley and Simon merged with an endless flow of pedestrians. When they reached the Strand, London's busiest thoroughfare, Hayley observed gentlemen in plumed hats and silk capes riding their mounts with reckless abandon, with little regard for those on foot.

Hayley's heels were being rubbed by the heavy shoes, but Simon moved on relentlessly. Carts and wagons, loaded with foreign products for the city's merchants, signaled their approach to the Thames River. Reaching the Red Lion Inn, Simon muttered, "I'm going to ask for lodgings here. Be sure to keep your hair covered with that cap, and don't say anything."

They entered the cobbled courtyard through an archway from the street, and Hayley stood to one side while Simon went to arrange for a room. The kitchen and public rooms occupied the main part of the building, and Hayley's nostrils caught the scent of roast beef wafting on the damp air. Her stomach groaned in protest.

Simon soon returned and motioned her to follow him up the stairs, where they entered a small room opening out on a wooden balcony. He breathed a sigh of relief as he sank to a rustic bench beside the lumpy bed.

"Now what?" Hayley questioned.

"I think you'll be safe enough here while I go for news. If our conspiracy has been discovered, I must learn the fate of the rest of our family. I can't make any plans until then. Will you be afraid to stay here by yourself for a few hours?"

"Probably, but do what you must," Hayley said wearily as she rubbed her blistered feet. "What difference does it make who rules England? I've tried to be obedient since this change in leadership seemed so important to the rest of you, but in truth, I'm tired of being a pawn in the political aspirations of others. All I want to do is settle down with my family."

My family? Do I still have a family? What of Father, and Robert, and little Roger? Uncle Simon had given no indication of their whereabouts. "Uncle Simon . . . ," she ventured, "what about Roger and—"

But he cut her short, without giving her the opportunity to finish. Turning fiercely toward her, his manner generated tremendous strength in spite of his small frame. "Don't say more! And I don't know what happened to Roger, though I have my fears about the possibilities. Tragedy has touched this family and its aspirations often enough. Your mother died before we could see her become Queen of England. Don't you entertain any idea of trying to foil our plans."

What are his plans when compared to the lives of three human beings? Hayley's amber eyes snapped, and she bit her tongue to quell a retort. Invoking Uncle Simon's wrath would serve no purpose and certainly would not ensure the safety of the others. And besides, she knew Simon Douglas believed women weren't supposed to have opinions; or if they did, they should keep them to themselves—one reason she would be pleased to be released from this political intrigue. As ruler of England she would still be subject to doing what the men of her family wanted.

"I'm hungry," she said, trying desperately to think of a subject that wouldn't foster an argument. "I haven't eaten much today."

"You'll have to stay hungry a bit longer. I'll bring you some food when I return. In the meantime, don't open this door for any reason. If we find that carrying out our plans is impossible, it may be necessary to send you to France. Your kinsmen there will look after you."

"But if King James has learned about me, I may never have the opportunity to return to England. I don't want to leave here without my family, or at least knowing what has been their fate. And I don't want to be harried as my grandmother was."

Simon cautiously opened the door and peered out. Apparently the way seemed clear, and motioning for her to bolt the door behind him, he disappeared.

Hayley paced around the room until her pent-up emotions settled. She rubbed her forehead and lifted the woolen cap from her head. The elaborate headdress was heavy, and she longed to have her hair hanging loosely around her shoulders. If only her maid were here with her soothing ministrations. Just imagining the long brush strokes that had become a nightly ritual relaxed Hayley, and she replaced the cap and peered out the window.

A sedan chair was borne into the courtyard on the shoulders of servants in matched livery. A gentleman and his lady stepped from the chair and entered the tavern room of the Red Lion. Horses carrying helmeted soldiers clattered over the cobblestones, and Hayley shrank back from the window. She stood in the center of the floor, poised for flight, her slender fingers at her throat. But where could she go? Uncle Simon had said to stay in the inn. When, after a reasonable time, no one tried the door, she decided the soldiers must not have been looking for her, or if so, they had been turned away.

Hayley finally lay down, fully clothed, on the uncomfortable bed, and pondered her situation. Her mother, Monique, as Uncle Simon had said, had been denied her rightful place as Queen of England. The daughter of Mary, Queen of Scots, and her third husband, the Earl of Bothwell, Monique had been secretly taken to France and reared in a convent, because of the turmoil in Scotland at the time of her birth. The common belief in Scotland was that Mary had miscarried the child. As a young woman Monique had returned to England incognito to marry Henry Douglas.

And Uncle Simon had correctly stated the intentions of his family to make Monique ruler of England when Queen Elizabeth died. But her own death, in 1602, had preceded that of Elizabeth by one year. James, Monique's half-brother, had a stronger claim to the throne than had eight-year-old Hayley, so the Douglases had had to admit defeat in their plans to control England.

At first Englishmen had thought James I might be a good king, lenient toward those of all religious faiths, but he soon proved himself an unpopular ruler. In disfavor with Parliament as well as the various religious factions in the country, James was disliked by most of his subjects. Hayley's family began scheming again, and she was helpless to prevent it. And to what end? Was she destined to forever flee for her life or be imprisoned, perhaps beheaded as her grandmother had been? If King James had now learned that he had a niece residing within his kingdom, and a threat to his throne, she doubted that her life would be worth much.

Although most of his subjects vilified King James because of his shambling gait, slavering mouth, and ungracious manners, Hayley was grateful to him for his sponsorship of a new translation of the Scriptures. No matter that the king's religious beliefs weren't her own, Hayley had studied the version of God's word now translated into the common language. Just yesterday she had committed another verse to memory.

"I will say of the Lord, He is my refuge and my fortress: my God; in him will I trust." When she had learned those words, she hadn't known how quickly she would need their truth to comfort her. With the assurance of the psalmist's words in her mind, Hayley placed her hand on the large cross of gold, set with diamonds and rubies, concealed on a chain inside her crude doublet.

Hayley's mind was at rest, but that didn't still the anguish of her heart, and she drenched the pillow with bitter tears. Although Hayley had been indoctrinated to believe that her duty to England must be placed above all else, nothing was worth having Roger a captive of her enemies. If she had known her family's ambitions would lead to this, duty or not, she would have revolted.

She knew she could submit to her grief only in private, for once Simon returned he would have no patience with "women's hysterics" as he would term her suffering. Hayley hoped that sleep would bring some relief, but she couldn't sleep, and dozing intermittently, she squirmed restlessly on the bed.

The soft rays of morning had infiltrated the drab room by the time Simon returned. A slight tap on the door awakened Hayley, and she moved as quietly as she could across the rough wooden floor.

"Simon," she heard, and recognizing her uncle's voice, she unlatched the door. He entered furtively, carrying a bundle and some food. The scent of the roasted meat didn't even tempt Hayley's appetite, for she couldn't sate her hunger until she knew the fate of her loved ones.

"Roger?" she asked breathlessly. Simon shook his head.

"The news is all bad. It seems that Robert was killed when they broke into the house, and your father and Roger were taken away. Best I can determine, they're imprisoned in the Tower. Apparently you are safe for the moment since your presence in London wasn't suspected. A troop of soldiers has been dispatched to Exeter, presumably to arrest you."

Hayley fell forward on the bed, and although sobs wrenched her body, she tried to smother her agony in the rough coverlet. At that moment she cared little for her own life, but for the sake of others, she wanted no sound to escape to the adjoining room. In such a short time her whole family had been taken from her. What reasons did she have for living?

"I'm afraid it's useless to pursue our plans at this time," Simon said wearily.

Hayley raised her head from the bed and regarded him with eyes wild with grief. "Is the throne of England worth our loss?"

Simon's brown eyes glistened with anger, and he clapped a hand over her mouth. "Quiet! Watch your tongue, and remember what you say or do may determine the fate of your father and Roger. Nothing is left to do but send you out of the country as quickly as possible. Their lives will be safe, I imagine, until the king finds out all the details."

"You're right, of course." Hayley sat up. Her grief was deep, but her body had needs as well. Her stomach protested at its emptiness, and Simon had brought food. She reached for a slab of roast mutton and some brown bread that at first seemed unpalatable, but Hayley ate it, knowing she would need strength.

"How were our plans discovered?" she asked her uncle. "Do you know?"

"A traitor in our midst!" he growled. "And apparently it was John Lawrence, the bloody hound."

"John Lawrence! Why, he's a neighbor!"

"Aye! But sometimes friends part over religion, and for years Lawrence has been a member of a group of dissenters. You wouldn't remember, but long ago his sister went out to America as a missionary to the natives. She perished along with the others in one of Raleigh's colonizing attempts. John likes neither Catholics nor

Puritans. I'll never forgive the scoundrel for what he's done to us now."

"Perhaps he wasn't the one. It's bad enough to have our plans disrupted, but to have a neighbor betray us makes it harder."

"Aye," Simon agreed, "so perhaps you'll do what's best and leave the country for a while."

"It's best to be forced out of my own country?"

Ignoring her words, Simon said, "I had hoped to send you to France, where you have at least visited, but no ships are going to the continent for several days. I have learned, however, that a boat leaves within a few hours for Virginia. I propose you leave on it."

"Leave here without seeing Father and Roger? And before I see Robert has a Christian burial? And why Virginia? It's nothing but wilderness!"

"You can't help your father or Roger, and Robert is dead . . . he'll be no less so if you remain in England," Simon said bluntly. "And going to Virginia could save your life. But it wouldn't be a permanent arrangement, just long enough to secure your safety. And you have a kinsman there—Jacques Guise, your mother's cousin, went out to Virginia in 1618 to work for the London Company. He's had more than a year to get established; no doubt he can give you shelter until calm returns to England. Guise's sister went with him, so you would have some feminine companionship. In a few months we should be able to arrange your return home; perhaps by then Roger and your father will have been released. I repeat . . . the best thing you can do to help your father and Roger is to leave the country as soon as possible. The *Jonathan* leaves before nightfall. Will you be on it?"

"Alone?"

Simon smiled slightly. "Oh, you won't be alone. The London Company is sending out ninety maidens to become brides of the men in their Virginia colony. One more woman won't be noticed, and if you conceal your identity and mingle with the other women, no one should recognize you."

Hayley bowed her head in her hands, tendrils of auburn hair disrupted during her restless slumber tumbling over her shoulders. Did Simon realize what he was asking? She would leave home and family, uninformed of whether or not they would live or die, unprepared for what Virginia might hold. All her life she'd depended on others and had been waited upon—making no decisions, doing no work. She'd been taught the duties of a queen, and had an education superior to any other woman of that time. But she had never before now had to use that education; now she was to be cast upon her own resources. No, not her own resources, alone. God was still her guide and protector through this troubled time. Encouraged by the thought, she lifted her head.

"I'll sail on the *Jonathan*."

Two hours later Hayley slipped out of her room at the Red Lion and mingled with the throngs heading toward the Thames. She didn't see Simon, for after he'd provided her with a satchel of clothes and some provisions for her journey, he had disappeared.

"I'll pay the captain your fare, and give him a letter to deliver to Jacques Guise, then I'll stay away from you," he had said. "Travel under the name of Hayley Douglas, and you should be safe enough."

Drawing a Bible from the satchel he'd brought her, Simon had continued, "Hayley, I can't emphasize enough the importance of secrecy. Despite this setback, we may still succeed with our plans. I want you to swear that you won't reveal your family background or our plans to anyone in America. This incident with John Lawrence should convince you that you can't trust anyone. Guise will know part of the story, but I'm sure he can be relied upon."

Hayley's hands had trembled as she placed them on the Bible, and she had hesitated before taking the vow. *But why could it possibly matter if I promise not to reveal my past to anyone in Virginia?* She had made the vow her uncle requested.

The wharf around the *Jonathan* was crowded with people, and Hayley eased in beside two women, trying to attract as little attention as possible. She compared her clothes with those of the other women and decided that Simon had chosen well. Her gray homespun dress flowed to the ground over a crinoline petticoat. Her reddish-brown wool cape, which was near the color of her concealed hair, provided enough warmth on the cloudy day. With one hand she clutched a shawl over her head, while with the other hand she held a satchel. Though the bundle was heavy with the added weight of the Bible, she had insisted that she must have one. Bumping against her legs, under her skirts, she felt the sack of gold coins Simon had forced upon her. He had cautioned her to allow no one to know that she carried them.

The crowd of women, chattering nervously, surged forward, and Hayley moved with them from the wharf, across a narrow plank to the ship's deck. One quick glance around the *Jonathan* filled her with despair. The main deck wasn't as large as the Great Hall at her home. How did Simon expect her to conceal gold coins, or anything else, in such a small, crowded area?

Hayley's thoughts were echoed by another young woman beside her.

"Gonna be bloody crowded, ain't it? All of us will have to sleep in that narrow, stuffy area below the main deck. As tall as you are, you won't be able to sit upright, much less stand up, but guess it will be worth it to get a new start in life."

"How long will the trip take?" Hayley asked her companion.

"Cap'n said six to eight weeks. Depends on the weather. Are you already promised to some settler in Virginia?"

Hayley glanced quickly at the dumpy blonde. For a moment, she had forgotten why these other women were going to Virginia. "No. No, I'm not promised."

"My Walter is waiting for me. He went out last year to work as a potter in Jamestown. He's saved enough to pay my passage. But you won't have any trouble finding a husband. Most of these other women ain't promised either, but I hear four hundred men over there will be waiting for this bride ship at the dock." With a pleasant smile that cheered Hayley, the girl added, "I'm Paula Reed."

Hayley scanned the wharf for a glimpse of Simon, sure he was watching from some point; however, her pulse quickened when she saw a familiar face in the crowd. She scanned her memory for a hint of his identity, and when she thought she recognized him as Arnold Wright, who had been her father's coachman at one time, she hurriedly dodged out of sight behind some rigging. She had been afraid of the man when she was a child, and the feeling remained. After a few minutes when she peered cautiously around the rigging, Wright was no place to be seen, and she hoped he had not seen her.

Paula Reed stood by Hayley's side when the *Jonathan* edged from its moorings, sails filling slowly as the boat headed down the Thames. Hayley's hands clutched the boat's rail as she strained her eyes to see the imposing battlements of the Tower of London. Her eyes misted until she couldn't see the outline of the medieval building, but in her thoughts, she penetrated the stone walls and bid a silent farewell to Roger and her father.

By the time the Tower had faded from view, and the open countryside of England fanned out on both sides of the boat, Hayley's hands felt numb, and she noted that her knuckles were white from her tense hold on the rail. The signet ring stood out vividly on her right hand. Simon had forgotten *that* when he had been removing every remnant of her past. She stared long at the ring, remembering all the things it symbolized. Surreptitiously she removed the ring, and when Paula wasn't watching, dropped it into the swirling water of the Thames.

Philip Lawrence observed the scene before him with amusement. The men of Jamestown were resplendent in their best velvet doublets and linen breeches. He had sensed the excitement when he had entered the village an hour before. No man paid any attention to Philip as he stood to one side, leaning against the rough wooden wall of the Jamestown church.

In dress, Philip looked much like the other men around him, but there the resemblance ended. His blue eyes contrasted vividly with his bronze skin and the long black hair that was tied in a queue at the nape of his neck. Tall and brawny, towering over the other men around him, Philip represented the best of both races—Indian and white—in his background. His strong face spoke of the earth, the forest, the vastness of the New World. A sardonic expression, tinged with sadness, lit his blue eyes as man after man passed by without a greeting.

Two men stopped before him, and Philip overheard their conversation.

"Here, fix this doublet for me, mate. First time I've had the bloody thing on since I came out to Virginia, and the ties are all twisted."

As he helped his friend with the garment, the other man asked, "Keen on gettin' a woman, be ye? What kind of woman be ye wantin'?"

"Don't matter. Been so long since I've wrapped me arms around a woman that I'd take a witch if that's all I can get."

As they moved on toward the James River, his companion glanced at Philip. "You could have taken an Indian woman, I reckon. It's been done."

"I'd just as soon sleep with a hog. I ain't that hard up for a woman."

Philip clenched his fists at the intended insult but stifled his urge to hit the man. He could achieve his future as a Virginia planter only if he lived peacefully with the residents of Jamestown, but he was learning that his goal to become an equal of the Englishmen was a hard one. His Indian father, Towaye, had warned him that it would be so, but Philip was determined.

23

Walking slowly toward the James, Philip could see the white sails of the English boat threading its way up the river. He wasn't interested in the women the *Jonathan* was bringing. He had come to Jamestown to contract for a servant, and he hoped some would be available on the boat. He had brought a hogshead of tobacco to pay the fare of a servant, and he wanted to be on hand when the passengers unloaded, so he could have his pick of the lot.

The man's remark about Indian women remained in Philip's mind. No longer did the uneasy truce the English had enjoyed with the Indians, further secured by the marriage of Powhatan's daughter, Pocahontas, to settler John Rolfe, seem to matter. And even after Pocahontas's death, the Indian chief had tolerated the English advances into his kingdom, but none knew better than Philip that the days of peace were almost over. Opechancanough, half-brother to Powhatan, was now the dominant leader among the coastland natives, and his hatred of the whites was well known. Watching the excitement of the men of Jamestown over the arrival of their prospective wives, Philip could feel nothing but fear for the safety of those women.

The deck of the *Jonathan* was crowded with women waving to the men, who surged forward as the ship, taking advantage of high tide, struck the sandy bank. The women seemed well dressed in spite of the many weeks at sea without adequate facilities for bathing and washing clothes. Cheering erupted as one voice from the settlers, and as soon as the women walked down the plank, overeager swains grabbed them.

"I'll take this one."

"The redhead's mine."

"I want the fat one. I need somebody to warm my bed next winter."

Guffaws greeted these sallies, and Philip experienced shame for his fellowmen. Some of the women were as bold as the men; others, shy and hesitant.

One girl shuddered when a rough hand caught her. "They told us we didn't have to choose right away. I ain't ready yet."

A plump blond woman called, "Walter! Here I am," and she rushed to meet a Jamestown youth who had apparently been expecting her. After kissing the young man, she turned toward the ship to help a tall slender woman who was groping her way down the gangplank. The woman's auburn hair hung limply around her shoulders, and her pale face was creased with lines of pain. The gray dress she wore was filthy, and she seemed too weak to hold the satchel that swayed loosely in her hand. When she reached the sandy beach, she collapsed.

The waiting men made no move to help her, and one observed, "I sure ain't wanting that woman. Look at her. Bet she don't live out the week. Nobody better spend his tobacco crop to pay *her* fare."

The blonde dropped to her knees beside the woman on the ground, who was murmuring piteously, *"Mon Dieu, aidez-moi."*

"Listen to that!" a man muttered. "Bloody Spaniard. Let's hope she dies . . . probably sent over here as a spy."

Philip shot a scornful look at the speakers. "She is not a Spaniard; she's speaking French."

"And where'd you learn your French, half-breed?" he was asked with a sneer. "In the wigwam?"

Philip refused to be needled. "From my mother," he answered calmly, and knelt beside the two women.

"Permettez-moi vous aider, Mademoiselle."

The auburn head moved to one side, but she didn't reply. Philip turned to the other woman. "What's the matter with her?"

"She's been sick for weeks. The voyage has been rough, and we've been eight weeks at sea. I don't know why she's speaking that language. She's English."

The man who was standing beside the young woman said, "Come on, Paula. I've been waiting for a year."

"But I hate to leave her. She's so nice, and I've been helping her."

Philip lifted the slack form into his arms and stood up. "I'll take her inside the fort. Perhaps someone will come to help her."

Paula handed Philip the woman's satchel, which he draped over his arm. "Her name is Hayley Douglas," Paula called as Walter hurried her away.

Despite the woman's long frame, her weight was so slight that Philip exerted no extra energy to carry her. Blood was oozing from her mouth, and when she retched, bloody excretion poured over her parched lips. Philip recognized the symptoms of scurvy, common to people too long on the ocean.

A rancid odor exuded from her body, and Philip was angry that the other women on the boat had allowed this sick woman to go unattended, while they donned their finery to attract men.

Near the fort the bargaining for wives was in full swing. One man held the hand of a woman. "I've got a house, two cows, and a flock of hens."

"Is that all?" she said with a laugh. "I've had a better offer than that already."

Inside the church, a minister was reading the wedding ceremony to several couples who had already made their decisions. Paula and Walter were among them.

A representative of the London Company was leading away a large group of women who had not yet made their choices and had demanded the protection promised them until they did.

Philip placed Hayley gently on the grass under the shade of an oak tree and felt her faltering pulse. This woman would die unless she had immediate care. Spring had come to Virginia already, and the hot, damp weather had turned the swampy area surrounding Jamestown into a steamy, unbearable spot. Philip's plantation was located on higher ground up country; if he could take her there, his mother could nurse her to health.

Philip looked around for some help, but only he had any interest in the sick woman. Philip had experienced enough shunning in his twenty-eight years to know what it was like to be ignored, and he muttered under his breath. A slight breeze wafted from the James, and Hayley's auburn hair flowed around her shoulders. With a tender touch, Philip lifted her hair and tucked it behind her head, fastening it away from her face with a comb that had become entangled in the limp tresses. Overcome with pity for the woman and moved by some other emotion that was new to him, Philip decided she wasn't going to die.

When he started to leave her, Hayley reached for his hand and held it weakly. He listened as she mumbled in a mixture of French and English. Most of the words were incoherent, but occasionally Philip understood a word. "Roger," seemed to be the most frequent word she uttered, but at one time, he heard her say "Father."

Since she apparently needed his presence, Philip was loath to leave her, but he hailed a councilor of the London Company who was passing by. The man paused, but his manner clearly indicated that he had no time for Philip.

"Sir, this woman is very ill. If she doesn't leave this area, she will die. May I have permission to take her to my home where my mother will nurse her?"

"You! Take this woman to your home? Certainly not!" Then when a glance revealed Hayley's condition, a crafty look came into the official's eyes. "You can take her if you have enough tobacco to pay her fare, but you have to marry her. You know these women came here to be married."

"Marry her!" Such a thought hadn't occurred to Philip. He took another look at Hayley, and despite her weak, untidy appearance, he detected an uncommon beauty. The thought of marrying an English woman appealed to him. Could this be God's will? Had this woman been delivered to his hands? Being the son of Maggie Lawrence, Philip had been taught that God looks after his own, and that nothing happens by accident.

Philip wasn't an impulsive man by nature, but he took another look at Hayley, and a thrill shook his large body. Gesturing toward a hogshead of tobacco stashed near the palisade, he said, "I'll take her." He could wait another year for an indentured servant.

The transaction made, Philip went in search of the minister. Reverend Brown wasn't at first responsive to the idea, but finally he told Philip to bring her into the church. Philip washed Hayley's face in an effort to revive her.

Hayley opened her eyes. *"Mademoiselle,"* he said.

Hayley shook her head. "No, not *mademoiselle,"* she murmured weakly.

"Yes, I forgot. I know you're English. Mistress Douglas then. You're very ill, and the only way you can receive proper care is for me to take you to my home. I'll be good to you."

This must be Jacques Guise, Hayley thought, and she nodded before she again lost contact with reality.

In the background, Hayley heard a man reading, and dreamily she repeated vows that had a familiar ring. What she was doing was wrong, her subconscious mind seemed to warn, but she was too weak to protest—just another man, making her decisions for her.

Hayley roused again in time to hear the minister say, "Hayley Douglas and Philip Lawrence, I pronounce you husband and wife together." The name "Lawrence" seared Hayley's memory, and she fainted.

chapter
2

THE WORLD WAS SHAKING AROUND HAYLEY, and over-head, through a slit in her eyelids, she could see the outline of treetops. Slowly opening her eyes, she gingerly moved her head from side to side, but even that slight effort sent pains charging through her head. At first she thought the movement she felt was occasioned by the rise and fall of the waves, but if she were still on the ship, she wouldn't have been surrounded by trees. No, she was in a crude cart, jolting along an uneven road. She could hear the labored breathing of an animal as it pulled the vehicle. The last thing she remembered was leaving the *Jonathan* at James-town. Where was she now?

As the cart moved from the dense forest into an open area, a sudden burst of sunlight caused Hayley's eyes to water. Abruptly, the vehicle plunged downhill, splashing into water, and the rough movement caused her stomach to churn. She coughed, and bitter secretion filled her mouth.

Immediately the movements stopped, and a dark-skinned stranger peered over the side of the vehicle. Hayley's senses reeled, and her mind struggled to establish some recollection of this man, as leaning toward her, he lifted her head and wiped away the bloody saliva that slipped from her mouth. His touch was tender, and Hayley leaned weakly against his sturdy shoulder when the retching eased.

"I remember you now. Weren't you the man who helped me at Jamestown?"

"Yes, I was at the riverside when the *Jonathan* arrived, and I carried you to the fort." He paused and peered keenly at her. "Is that *all* you remember about today?"

"I remember very little about the last several weeks. I've hardly ever been ill before, but those days on the ship almost killed me. I don't know what's wrong with me."

"You have scurvy, a disease that often plagues those who spend many days on the ocean."

Hayley glanced at his dark face. His high cheekbones and slightly slanted eyes appeared foreign to her. "Am I going to die?"

A smile lit his deepset blue eyes. "Not if I can help it, and I think I can. Once we arrive at my home, I'll send for my mother. She will know how to care for you."

"Are you Jacques Guise?"

The man hesitated. "No, my name is Philip Lawrence."

"Then what happened to Jacques Guise? He's my mother's kinsman, and I was supposed to go to his home. Why am I with you?"

Philip lowered her into a comfortable position in the cart.

"There was no one to meet you at the boat, and when I saw how ill you were, I decided to take you with me. Jamestown is no place for a sick person. A blond woman told me your name."

"Paula Reed. She was very helpful to me on the ship."

"I'm going to stop for the night in about an hour, but do you think you could eat something now?"

Hayley's stomach rejected the idea, and she gagged. "Oh, no, I can't stand the thought of eating."

"That's because you haven't had anything except salt pork and moldy bread for days." Philip disappeared for a moment, and when he returned he carried a wooden bowl of fruit.

"Strawberries!" Hayley said. "The strawberries weren't even blooming when we left England. Is it spring already?"

"Spring comes early in Virginia. Our strawberry season is almost over, but I've been watching as we've traveled, and I found a few."

He lifted her to a sitting position and placed the bowl in her lap. "Why not lean against the back of the cart and eat as we move along? Eat slowly . . . just a few at a time." Hayley stretched out her legs, but every movement brought a grimace of pain to her face.

"My whole body feels bruised, and it even hurts to eat," she commented as she placed the first berry in her mouth. "My teeth and gums are sore."

"You'll soon be well if you eat plenty of fresh fruits and vegetables. I think I can find enough food to tempt your appetite."

Wonderingly, Hayley looked at him. "Why are you so concerned about me?"

Philip had no answer, and moving to the front of the cart, he picked up a goad and gave a command to the ox, and it moved forward. Sitting as she was at the back of the cart, Hayley could watch their progress.

They moved through a treeless area crisscrossed with small streams. The area was apparently swampy, and it was rough going for the ox, whose hoofs sank deeply into the mire. Tall reeds reached to Philip's neck, but his wide shoulders parted the weeds as though they were nothing. Hayley admired his determined actions. The ox did his bidding without protest.

Hayley luxuriated in the warm sun spreading around her, the heat bringing a sense of renewal to her emaciated body. A gentle breeze carried with it a scent of the ocean, as well as a tangy smell she was unable to identify until she spotted a grove of evergreens ahead of them. The path of the sun as it slowly lowered toward the horizon told Hayley they were traveling westward.

Why am I so calm? Hayley pondered. Here she was, wandering around in the American wilderness with a strange man, without any hint of destination. She reminded herself that she was in her present condition because of a man by the name of Lawrence. But she saw nothing to fear from her companion, who often turned toward her with an encouraging smile. By the time he stopped the cart again, the strawberries were gone.

"We'll camp here for the night. It's only a short distance to my home, but more travel isn't good for you."

"Where is your home, Master Lawrence?"

"About ten miles east of Jamestown, along the James River. For the past year I've been trying to establish a tobacco plantation."

"And before the past year? When did you arrive from England?"

He gave her a strange look, Hayley thought, but he

didn't answer. He reached his hand toward her. "Why don't you try to walk a bit? I'll help you."

Hayley slid with effort to the edge of the cart, and took his hand. Her skirt slipped above her knees, and when she tried to cover her legs, Philip gently tucked the garment around her ankles. When her quivering legs touched the ground, she staggered, but Philip's arms circled her slender waist immediately. "Hold on to me. Being on a boat for several weeks without exercise would have weakened you, even if you hadn't been ill."

As she leaned against him, Philip marveled that her head came to his shoulders. He had never seen such a tall woman before. His own mother was small, as were all the other English women who had arrived in the Virginia colony.

"Oh, I'm ashamed of being so weak. Believe me, I'm not usually such a burden."

Moving back and forth with Hayley along the creek bed, Philip touched the sharp thrust of her ribs through the linen dress. A few weeks of good food would take care of that. The eruptions of her breath in short gasps told him she had exercised enough, and he tenderly lowered her to the ground where she leaned weakly against a tree.

Quickly igniting a fire with a flint he drew from a pocket, Philip placed a clay pot on the coals and poured liquid into it. Hayley watched his deliberate movements, and although he didn't seem to hurry, he accomplished much in a short time.

He was dressed simply in a brown linen shirt and baggy knee-length breeches. Woolen stockings extended above his bulky leather boots. Black hair, which grew to a point on his forehead, was pulled back and tied with a black ribbon.

"Here, drink this," Philip interrupted her musings by holding a small clay pot before her. A bitter aroma exuded from the steaming liquid.

"What is it?" Hayley asked, suddenly suspicious of him. After all, his name was Lawrence. Could her enemies have followed her to America?

"Just some herbs boiled in water. This will settle your stomach and help you to rest. You can trust me; I won't give you anything harmful."

She searched his eyes. But what choice did she have? She knew no one else in the whole colony of Virginia. She drank the nasty brew, coughing and sputtering as it went down.

His smile was tender. "I know they're bitter; my mother has made me drink a lot of this brew."

"You say your mother will nurse me?"

"Yes. She was born in England, but she's learned many of the medicines available in our forests."

"I didn't think any English women were here."

"Yes, several even before the *Jonathan* brought so many of you."

"Was Paula's young man at the dock to meet her? She was eager to see him again."

"Yes, he was there," Philip answered as he busied himself at the fire. "He's the potter in Jamestown . . . seems like a competent workman."

Hayley ate more strawberries that Philip brought her but she refused the gruel he stirred over the fire for his own supper.

"Where am I going to sleep?" she asked. "I must lie down."

"You had better sleep in the cart, for you shouldn't lie on the ground. I have a coverlet to keep you warm. But would you like to wash a bit before you sleep?"

"Oh, yes, please. I am so dirty. My clothes are filthy, for we weren't allowed to do any washing on board the ship. They even rationed our drinking water, as rancid as it was. It was a miserable trip. I've crossed the English channel to France several times, and I was foolish enough to think crossing the Atlantic would be no worse than that. What was your experience coming across the ocean?"

Without looking at her, Philip answered, "I was born in America, and I've never sailed on the ocean."

But the first English hadn't settled at Jamestown until 1607, just thirteen years ago. He couldn't have been born to any of those settlers, for he had to be several years older than she. Yet he said his mother was English!

When Philip carried a bowl of water to her, she said, "If you would bring my satchel, I believe there's a small cloth in it I can use for sponging."

Philip placed the satchel beside her and turned his back to afford her some privacy while she bathed. He was eating a bowl of gruel when he heard sobbing, and he turned toward her. Her hands lay limply at her side.

"I didn't realize how weak I was. I can't even wring out the cloth."

Hesitantly Philip approached her. "If you will allow me to help . . ."

Startled, Hayley gazed upward. He did not meet her eyes, and his solemn face indicated that he knew how preposterous the suggestion was.

"I would appreciate your help. Perhaps my hands, face, and throat could be freshened."

It seemed that Philip's face took on a more dusky tint, as without looking at her, he sponged her face. Hands, so competent at his other tasks, trembled as his fingers caressed the curve of Hayley's face, removing the grime to reveal a shiny, pearl-like sheen.

He gently loosened the buttons at the collar of her dress, but a heavy gold chain was in his way, and he pulled it free from her bodice. Hayley grabbed at the chain, but she wasn't quick enough to prevent exposing the gold cross set with diamonds and rubies.

She wordlessly slipped the cross back inside her bodice, and Philip concentrated instead on washing her neck and throat. Hayley searched for an explanation to make about the cross. She knew such elaborate jewels did not match the humble clothing she wore. Would he think she had stolen it? She decided silence was better than a lie.

The silence prevailed until they heard rapid steps approaching through the forest. Stepping to the cart, Philip lifted a musket from it. Shielding Hayley with his body, he waited.

A lone man charged into the clearing. "Where ees she? Vot 'ave you done wif her?"

Philip lifted the gun. "Who are you? Explain yourself?"

"*Je m'appelle Jacques Guise.* Where my cousin is? The letter I get and go to fin' her and learn you 'ave taken her away."

Hayley tried to struggle to her feet, and Guise saw her. "Ah, there is you. Why 'ave you come away wif thees man?"

Guise rushed to her and dropped to his knees, kissing her on both cheeks. "The child of my cousin, Monique. I greet you. You fin' a welcome wif me. We leave now."

Philip pulled Guise roughly away from Hayley. "She won't go any place with you. I married this woman at the Jamestown church today. She's mine."

With a cry, Hayley half-rose from her reclining position, and her face mirrored the surprise on Guise's countenance.

"Marry her," Guise shouted, and in his anger, his English seemed to improve. "Why, you . . . you . . . you're nothing but a redskin. How dare you marry this woman? Don't you know she's—"

"No," Hayley shouted, mustering all the strength she possessed. Guise must not reveal her identity.

Philip took Guise's arm and propelled him away from Hayley. "You have little room to speak of another's ancestry. You can't even speak the English language. Get out. The lady stays with me."

Guise, a squat man with an impressive mustache and a pointed beard, sputtered, "Ees thees true, *mademoiselle*? 'Ave you truly wed thees man?"

Hayley tried to struggle to her feet but fell backward. "I don't know. I've been ill for weeks on the boat, and I don't remember too well what has happened. I have a faint recollection of being in a ceremony of some kind."

She looked at Philip, whose dark face was partially obscured by the gathering dusk. She hadn't noticed before the sweep of jaw that hinted of aggressiveness and stubbornness. The look of truth was on his face, and she didn't doubt his word. This man was her husband.

"We were married today," he repeated. "Ask the minister at the church; ask the official of the London Company who took my hogshead of tobacco for her passage."

"But my fare was already paid," Hayley protested weakly.

"Guise, this woman is ill, and she needs rest. Be on your way."

"I vil go, but I keep in touch, *ma cousine*."

Guise slowly disappeared into the darkness. Dropping to his knees beside Hayley, Philip said, "Let me help you to the cart. You've had too much excitement."

Hayley gave herself over to his care. If what he said was true, did she have any choice? His touch was tender as he lifted her upward, and when she stood beside him with knees that refused to stop trembling, she was thankful for his strength.

"Is it true what he said? Are you an Indian?"

Philip turned away impatiently, and his indignant gesture answered her query. "My father is an Algonquian, but my mother is English. Why must half my ancestry blight what I am today? Inside I feel English. Does it make that much difference who my father was?" Hayley started to speak, but he hurried on, "What a man does with his life is more important than his blood ties. I'm going to become a great man in this colony or die in the effort."

Hayley leaned wearily against him. "I don't know that it makes any difference to me who you are. You've been kind to me, and I appreciate it. I've always contended that God looks upon all people with the same consideration. Perhaps this will be a good time for me to prove if I really mean what I say." She paused to catch her breath, for speech was becoming more and more difficult. "But a marriage between us is impossible, and that has nothing to do with your ancestry. I'm in no position to take a husband." Her energy spent, she pitched forward; but Philip caught her before she reached the ground.

chapter

3

STRONG WAVES WERE FLOWING OVER HAYLEY, and she experienced the sensation of rising from the depths, only to sink again. Roger was floating helplessly beside her, and she kept trying to hold his small head above water, but he slipped from her grasp. Plunging beneath the water to find him, she screamed, "Roger! Roger, come to me." At last she was buoyed upward to the surface of the water, and she breathed deeply as the waves became calm and soothing.

Hayley opened her eyes to see the face of a woman before her—a face framed with golden hair, streaked with gray, with blue eyes gleaming from a lined face, still beautiful in middle age.

"Come, Philip," the woman said in an accent that was definitely English. "She's awakened."

A man knelt beside her, and Hayley recognized him, as the scene with Jacques Guise infiltrated her mind with startling intensity. She was married to this man, who smiled affectionately at her.

"Welcome back," he said. "For a while we thought you would leave us. Are you feeling better?"

"I don't know. The last thing I remember, you were leading me to the cart. Where am I now?"

"That was more than a week ago. You're at my home, and my mother has been helping you to get well."

The woman appeared at the edge of the bed with a small bowl. "Try to sit up, Hayley, and drink some of this broth. We've given you herbed water, but that's all the nourishment you've had."

Philip put his arms under Hayley's shoulders and lifted her to a sitting position. She winced at the movement for her whole body was sore to the touch. They didn't have to tell her how near death she had been; her limp fingers couldn't even grasp the spoon, so Philip's mother fed her small spoonfuls of the savory liquid.

Once the broth was eaten, Hayley knew she did feel better, and she looked around the room. She was lying on a feather mattress on a wooden bed. On one side of the room a low fire burned, and above a stone hearth two iron pots hung on a metal bar. Bearskin rugs lay on the wooden floor of the sparsely furnished room. Two benches surrounded a long table set with various pieces of pewterware, and a chest with a chipped mirror was the only other piece of furniture. Clumps of dried herbs hung from the wooden rafters, permeating the room with aromatic scents. In one corner, near the fireplace, a ladder gave access to a loft above the single room. Although the furnishings were crude and sparse, the room was homey and peaceful.

Glancing down at her body, Hayley realized she had been bathed and her garments had been changed, for she no longer wore the soiled linen dress from her arrival in Jamestown. No doubt Philip's mother had performed the service for her. Quickly touching her neck, she found that the gold cross was intact.

Philip said, "My mother's name is Maggie Lawrence; she bathed you and put on your clean garments. She looked in your satchel for the clean clothes, but we haven't bothered anything else."

Hayley could feel the weight of the gold coins braced against her thigh, and she thought he was probably assuring her that they hadn't taken the money. Nodding her head, she reached a hand to the older woman.

"Thank you for caring for me. I would have died otherwise, I'm sure."

"It's been over thirty years since I made the trip from England to America, but I still remember the seasickness I experienced. No other illness can compare to that discomfort."

"You've been here that long?"

"Yes, I came in 1587 with Raleigh's colonists."

"But I've always understood that all of them perished."

A hint of bitterness was reflected in Mistress Lawrence's light laughter. "I may be the only one left now, but many of us were alive and hearty for a long time. I didn't live with the main group of colonists in their village near the Chowan River, for I married my Algonquian husband and lived in his village. But you'd better wait and hear that story at another time. You're still not completely recovered."

"Oh, please tell me. I'm all right. Weak, maybe, but definitely on the mend."

Philip nodded to his mother, and with sadness mirrored on her face, she said, "Our people were prospering nicely, but not long before the settlers came to Jamestown, Powhatan, leader of the local tribes, and his warriors massacred the English."

"It isn't safe for the English here?" Hayley felt the color draining from her face.

Philip sat down on one of the benches, stretching his long legs in front of him. "That is probably true, although apparent peace has reigned since John Rolfe and Pocahontas were married. Pocahontas was Powhatan's daughter. You know who I mean?"

"I surely do," Hayley replied. "I saw Pocahontas when she was in our country. All England was talking about her."

A cool breeze wafted through the house, and Hayley asked, "Do you think I'm able to walk around a bit? My whole body feels stiff and sore."

Supported by Philip and his mother, Hayley walked to the open doorway. About a mile away, a wide river appeared as placid as a lake.

"Is it the same river that flows past Jamestown?"

"Yes," Philip answered, and Hayley noted a tinge of pride in his voice. "I chose this spot for my home because it commanded a view of the James."

"But I don't understand. If I remember, I thought that Raleigh's colony was far south of Jamestown. What is your family doing here?"

Maggie Lawrence answered. "A plague struck and killed most of the residents of Winnetoon where we lived, and we decided to move to the English village. We arrived there a few days after the place was destroyed. We lived with the Pamunkey tribe for several years, until we became disturbed over the leader's attitude toward the English."

She hesitated, and exchanged glances with her son. Hayley deduced that she omitted part of the story when she continued, "A few years ago we heard that the House of Burgesses was awarding land to 'old' settlers . . . those who had lived in Virginia for a long period of time. No one had a longer record than I, but I wasn't sure the Burgesses would accept it. Philip had it in his head to become a planter, so we applied for land, which was given to us."

"Do you live here, too?" Hayley asked hopefully.

"No, Towaye, my husband, does not like to live close to others. We built our home farther back in the forest, and left the river land to Philip. That way, we're all happy."

Each day Hayley could note an improvement in her health, but her clothes still hung loosely on her frame, and the high bust, one of the many characteristics she had inherited from her famous grandmother, had dwindled considerably. Even the distorted mirror atop the walnut chest in the corner showed her face to be pale and thin.

Philip would leave the house early each morning and return at sunset, tired and dirty from his long hours in the tobacco fields. But, in his absence, Hayley soon formed a close companionship with his mother. Maggie Lawrence, so long separated from her country, was eager to learn about changes in England. Although she seemed perfectly content in her buckskin garments, still she fingered each item of Hayley's clothing and asked dozens of questions about current European fashion.

"The women's garments are beautiful, but not very comfortable," she assured her mother-in-law. "Of course, for this overseas journey, I wore plain garments, but at home, the well-dressed lady wears a roomy chemise under her gown, as well as stockings made of various cloths, and leather corsets to encase her body in strong lacings. Of course, the farthingale is still used some, although the size is much smaller than in my mother's day, and many petticoats under velvet or silk gowns are more fashionable now. You would have worn the farthingale, I suppose?"

"Oh, yes, a lady wasn't supposed to display her true figure." The older woman ran rough hands over her pliable buckskin garment. "These clothes might not be fashionable, but they are comfortable. However, there are times when I long to be dressed in silks and linens again. I notice that the gentry in Jamestown still wear ruffs."

"Yes, and the women, too. I believe that the ruffs aren't quite as elaborate as in the days of Queen Elizabeth though. But men's clothes have changed a lot; their doublets and breeches are styled much as always, but the garments are made of silk, velvets, damasks, or taffetas. The most costly items are even edged with furs."

"And I can remember when such garments were worn only by kings." Maggie Lawrence shook her head in wonder. "Hard to believe that so much could have changed in such a short time. Even the ruler of England is different, I hear. Queen Elizabeth was ruling when we set sail for America. How long ago did she die?"

"Oh, a long time ago. I was just a child, but I remember the days of mourning for her. The present ruler, James, is a cousin of hers. You would remember that she never married."

"Right before we left England, Mary, Queen of Scots, a contender for the throne, was imprisoned because she had participated in a plot to assassinate the queen. What happened to her?"

Sweat moistened Hayley's palms, and a tremor shook her body. She hoped it had gone unnoticed, but already she had learned that little escaped the keen blue eyes of this woman.

"Queen Elizabeth was afraid of Mary, fearing she would take the throne, so she had the Scot Queen beheaded." She had heard the story often enough, and the details were vivid in Hayley's mind.

"Goes to show it doesn't pay to oppose the ruler of England, I guess," Philip said, joining them for his evening meal.

Hayley didn't answer, but she stood so quickly her head swam. She walked to the door for a breath of air, and felt Philip's questioning gaze upon her.

"Why did James become the ruler?" Mistress Lawrence inquired as she busied herself putting food on the table.

Forcibly controlling her emotions, Hayley turned back into the house. "James was Mary's son and probably had the best claim to the throne. Elizabeth more or less willed him the kingdom, probably because she felt conscience-stricken over killing his mother."

"Didn't Mary have any other children?"

Would they never stop questioning her? *How can I tell them anything more without revealing my ancestry?* Because of their kindness she felt she owed them some sort of an answer. But were theirs innocent questions? How much did these two people already know about her? Perhaps she had given away some secrets during the days of illness.

"Mary was with child several times, but the general opinion seems to be that James is the only one of her children who grew to adulthood." That explanation would have to do. She wasn't going to lie, and she had taken a vow!

"What about the religious conflicts in Europe? When I left, our small band of dissenters was in the middle of the conflict between the Catholics and the Church of England. We had hoped to start a mission work among the natives and eventually move our whole congregation here so we could worship in freedom. But the failure of Raleigh's colonizing effort stopped that."

"I suppose you know that Sir Walter Raleigh was also executed."

"Yes, Philip heard that in Jamestown. By the way, what religion does the new king follow?"

"He's Protestant, and most Catholics feared his coming to power, but religion doesn't seem to make any difference to those who dislike him. He's unpopular with most everyone."

"What about the chance of overthrowing him?" Philip asked, as he washed the grime from his face and hands. "Have there been any attempts?"

"The king may have his faults," Hayley said in an effort to divert their attention, "but he has accomplished some worthwhile things." She went to her satchel and lifted out the heavy Bible. "A few years ago he sponsored a new translation of the Bible into the language of the common people, and it's an improvement over the Geneva Bible. I think you would enjoy reading this."

Hayley carried the Bible to Mistress Lawrence, who reached for the volume with eager fingers. "How wonderful! Our only Bible is in tatters. I've used it for years to teach children to read, and we've also read it before bedtime each night. The original cover has been replaced by deerskin several times. It will be such a pleasure to read this one."

Pleased to have something to share with this woman who had saved her life, Hayley said, "When I go back to England, I'll leave this for you to read. They're not plentiful, but I can always find another one."

Conscious of the shocked silence, Hayley looked from one, whose face registered disappointment, to the other, whose blue eyes registered surprise. Face flushed, Hayley stammered, "I mean *if* I return to England someday, I'll leave it for you."

Since childhood Hayley had been told that her destiny and political legacy were of supreme importance. And she knew her father and Simon well enough to know they wouldn't let her disregard that heritage, but would this marriage to Philip disrupt their plans?

After supper Philip asked, "Why not read it aloud, Mum?" when she reached again for the Bible. He stretched out on a bearskin near the door to catch the cool westward breeze. "The thing I miss most about living alone is being unable to share the Bible reading with you and Father at night. Now that Hayley has brought a Bible into our home, I can read it for myself."

Our home. He must still consider their marriage valid. What would marriage to this man involve? When they were alone—when his mother had left, as she surely would in a few days—would she be expected to fulfill the duty of a wife?

Maggie Lawrence turned to the last chapter of Matthew, and after reading Jesus' closing words to his disciples, she closed the Bible, and the faraway gleam in her eyes made Hayley wonder if this woman, who seemed serene and confident now, had once experienced the frustration and pain that Hayley knew because of separation from her family?

But her words showed no trace of sadness. "Ah! The comfort of those words . . . the last ones my father read before I left for America. 'And, lo, I am with you always, even unto the end of the world.'"

She shook her head as if coming out of a dream and turned to Hayley. "What part of England do you come from?"

Hayley hesitated perceptibly, and again she sensed Philip's watching eyes. But what could it possibly matter if they knew where she had lived? "I was born in London and lived there until eight years ago, when I moved to the countryside of Devon . . . near Exeter."

"Devon! Why, that was my home, too, but of course, I would have been gone before you were born. Perhaps you know my family though . . . Alfred and Mary Lawrence were my parents. Do you know them?"

"No, I don't believe so." Hayley searched her brain for some way to stop this conversation. She could plead the desire to go to bed, but if she did that, they would have to retire also.

"Perhaps you know my brother, John Lawrence."

Hayley's senses blurred, and a faintness enveloped her. *John Lawrence's sister! I am married to John Lawrence's nephew.* Was this a plot? Had they deliberately kidnapped her? Had Philip really married her, or was that just a ruse to keep her in sight until he could send her back to England?

She didn't realize she was swaying in the chair until Philip rushed to her, but she made an effort to overcome the swoon. She must not let them know she was suspicious of them.

Hayley glanced up at Philip and spoke with a calm she didn't feel. "I'm all right now . . . just a faint spell." Then she turned to Maggie Lawrence. "I've heard of your brother, for he lived in the same area where we did. I'm sure he's alive and well." Perhaps that would satisfy them, for she didn't want to admit the man had been a close neighbor.

"I'm happy to hear that. Someday I'd like to contact my brother, for he's believed me to be dead all these years. But I hesitate to do so, for he probably wouldn't approve of my lifestyle now." She stood up and placed the Bible on top of the chest. "But we've kept you up too long. We will have more time to talk tomorrow. Philip, I think you should send word to your father that I'm ready to come home. In a few days Hayley will be able to do without me."

Long after Philip had climbed the ladder to the loft, and his mother had stretched out on the sleeping mat, Hayley lay awake. Through the open window she heard a nightingale calling to its mate, and the sound echoed the loneliness in her heart. How she missed home and family. How she worried for the safety of her father and little Roger.

Should she try to slip away some night and go to Jacques Guise to ask for his protection? Unaccustomed as she was to making decisions, the burden lay heavy upon her. Was Philip in league with her enemies in England?

No, she decided, she would stay where she was, although she knew that could also present problems. If she settled down here as Philip's wife, what would she do when the summons came to return to England? And she knew it would come. One way or another, her uncle would send for her. Already Hayley had a strange reluctance to leave Philip.

The next day the two women walked toward the forest, the farthest distance Hayley had ventured from the house, and she discovered that her legs were still weak and trembly. Would she ever regain her health? She savored the smell of evergreens and the scent of the James River, which wafted toward them by the west wind. At the edge of the forest, they sat on a fallen log.

"You mustn't journey away from the house by yourself, Hayley. You're safe enough here in the clearing, but keep in sight of Philip at all times."

"But I thought it was peaceful here now," Hayley answered with some surprise.

"On the surface it appears so, but since Powhatan's death, his brother Opechancanough controls the tribes, and he's sown seeds of hatred. Even my son, Saponi, hates the English and is determined they shall be driven from these shores."

"Saponi! You have another son?" Strange that fact hadn't been hinted before.

"Yes, and he's all Indian, just as much as Philip wants to be all English. The two do not get along well, and they never have. It worries Towaye and me . . . one of the disadvantages, we've learned, of trying to mix cultures."

Hayley reached for her hand. "Tell me, have you ever been sorry that you married him? Maybe I shouldn't ask, but I have wondered. You seem so happy."

A tender smile played around the older woman's lips. "It hasn't been easy, and at times I've longed for England and my family. I've never won complete acceptance from *his* people, but Towaye has never disappointed me. He's always been my love, and the years haven't changed that." She gripped Hayley's hand tightly. "I've wanted to say this to you, child, but I've hesitated. It won't be easy for you either, for I suspect your lifestyle in England was far superior to mine. You'll have bad days when you want to throw up your hands and flee, but if you give Philip a chance, he'll make you happy. Even though he is determined to become an English gentleman, he is very much like his father. You won't be disappointed."

"I've already learned that Philip is a kind and caring man," Hayley said, remembering his help on the journey from Jamestown. She grew uncomfortably warm when she recalled his bathing of her face and arms.

"And let me tell you now how pleased I am that Philip found you. If you hadn't come, he would have married an Indian girl. I feared he would always be seeking a love he wouldn't find with her but he's safe with you."

While Hayley sought to frame a response to that disturbing comment, Maggie Lawrence continued her reverie, "As the years have gone by, I've been distressed sometimes, thinking I may have failed in my main purpose for coming to America. I had come as a missionary, but frankly, I haven't seen much fruit from my labor."

"Oh, surely you've won some people to Christ."

"Yes, Towaye and Philip are both dedicated Christians, and there are others, for I've told dozens of people about my Jesus. Some have listened; some have not. The people often pay more attention to what Towaye says about his faith than the words I have for them." With a lilt of laughter in her voice, she continued, "Tomorrow he should be here, and after more than thirty years of marriage, I can hardly wait to see him."

With frequent glances toward the door, she hurried to provide extra food for their meals. "Surely I have cooked enough to take care of you until you feel like doing the housework."

Hayley didn't answer. Maggie must be distressed with Hayley's lack of effort to help with the work after her health returned. Well, the woman would just have to think she was lazy, rather than ignorant of how to work. All her training had been directed toward *ruling,* not toward menial service.

As she had watched the other woman capably perform the household chores, milk the goats, and feed the chickens, Hayley assessed her personal work qualities. She could play the lute. But where in Virginia could she find a lute? The whole colony probably didn't contain a musical instrument, and if she did find one, who would have time to listen? She could do fine embroidery, but where in Virginia would she find the necessary materials? She could read and write, but she didn't see one book in the house, nor any paper or pens. No, her training would prove worthless in a Virginia household. Philip had truly made a poor choice of a wife when he had chosen her.

Hayley's fingers twitched nervously. She knew Philip would expect her to take over the household duties, and she had no idea what she could do. Surreptitiously she had observed Maggie's movements, hoping she might learn something.

Standing at the dresser and peering into the mirror, trying to make her hair behave, she heard a slight sound at the doorway. Through the mirror Hayley saw the tall form of a man blotting out the daylight.

"Towaye," Maggie Lawrence cried and ran into his wide-swung arms; their lips met in a passionate caress.

"Oh, my Maggie," he whispered in tones strangely like Philip's. "How I have missed you! The days have been long, the nights endless."

Laughter shook his wife's voice as she nestled closer to him. "I know, my husband. I had thought that after all these years it might not be so, but my love for you and the ties that bind us are stronger than ever before."

"While you've been away, I thought of those times many years ago when you ran away and left me."

"But I always came back, Towaye . . . always knew you were for me, even when I tried to deny it."

He kissed her again, and Hayley realized that they didn't even know she was in the room. She noted that Towaye was every bit as tall as Philip, although he was more slender. His buckskin garments hung gracefully over a straight back and muscular shoulders.

The reunited couple looked long into each other's eyes, and Hayley turned away. She had never before witnessed such strong attraction and love.

Wouldn't it be wonderful to have a man love me that much? The men in Hayley's family had valued her because of the political power she could bring them. She had never been deluded into thinking they loved her for herself.

55

"My husband, come, you must meet our new daughter." She led Towaye toward Hayley.

Dark brown eyes surveyed her searchingly as he bowed slightly. "My Philip should have an English woman. It is good. You are welcome in our family." Turning to Maggie Lawrence, he said, "I have talked to Philip in the field and told him we would be on our way. Do you have some food we can carry with us? I want to be home by nightfall."

The glow kindled by Towaye's arrival had not yet left his wife's face, and her laugh was young and carefree. She lifted a deerskin bag from the hearth. "I knew you would be eager to leave, so I prepared a pack before you came. As soon as I gather my few personal possessions, I'll be ready."

chapter

4

HAD SHE EVER BEEN ALONE BEFORE? Since her father had suspected that enemies might try to take her life, Hayley had always been carefully guarded. Now she was destined to spend day after day alone in this small room. Why, it wasn't as big as her bedroom in their manor house at Exeter! Although she reminded herself that this was just a temporary existence, still she wanted to be useful.

Tallying the chores, Hayley tried to judge how much time she had before Philip came in for the night. The outside work should be completed first.

Peering anxiously out the door, Hayley lifted a small woven basket and headed toward the fence that enclosed the flock of chickens. Mistress Lawrence had scattered the grain on the ground and gathered the eggs in a few minutes, but when Hayley took some corn and swung her arm wide, nothing scattered except the chickens, which flew wildly to the far side of the pen. The grain fell to the ground on the outside of the enclosure.

Her next effort was better, and when the frightened chickens ran to pick up the grain, she hurried to the other side of the pen. Reaching through the slats in the fence she drew six eggs from the nests. One of them crashed to the ground, splattering egg yolk on the bottom of her dress, but the others she carried safely to the house.

Hayley looked toward the fence surrounding the two goats a long time before she finally picked up a wooden bucket and moved toward the animals. She had never before attempted to milk a goat, although she had watched Philip's mother perform the task several times, now was as good a time as any to learn. She lifted her hand to the hinge on the gate several times before she mustered the courage to go inside. Walking slowly toward the nanny goat, she said soothingly, "Good day, goat. I'm not afraid of you."

But her good courage proved in vain. She touched the goat with a quivering hand, and that was the last time she came in reach of either animal. Again and again she followed them around the pen, and when she finally gave up, she was dismayed at her appearance. Her shoes were encrusted with grime; her dress tail, filthy. Well, at least she had a clean dress to change into, but as she hurried toward the house, she was distressed to note how far the sun had traveled to the west.

"No time to change clothes now," she said, as she tied a fresh apron over her dress. Kneeling beside the fireplace, she gasped. The fire had gone out; she'd forgotten to place any wood on it. Hurriedly she piled a few sticks of wood on the dead coals and blew on them as she'd seen her mother-in-law do. Ashes billowed around her head, and as she coughed and waved them away, she heard a step at the door.

Turning suddenly, she moaned, "Oh, is it time for supper already?"

"I came in early to help you."

"I've let the fire go out," Hayley said with tears in her voice. "And I wanted to have your supper ready when you came in."

Philip took a flint from the mantle, knelt beside her, and soon had the flame going. "It isn't time to eat yet."

"And I couldn't milk the goat either . . . couldn't even get close to her," Hayley said with averted eyes.

He touched her shoulder. "I don't expect you to do all this work. It's too much for you."

"Your mother worked."

"Yes, but Mums are like that. Remember I've been living here alone and have had all the work to do. You take care of heating our food, and I'll milk the goat."

"But I want to help you too, Philip." Hayley tried to keep the tremor from her voice, but she didn't, and her chin trembled.

Philip touched her cheek tenderly. "You can help me by staying healthy and keeping me company. I don't mind doing all the work, so wash your face. I'll be in soon."

Hayley peered in the mirror after he left, and was shocked to see how dirty she was. If she couldn't do anything else, she could at least present a pleasant appearance, so she hurriedly sponged off her face and removed the soiled clothing. She donned her nicest gown, a pale blue linen with a white chemise, and a small ruff at the neckline.

Glancing frequently at the door, she hurried to complete her toilet before Philip returned. Her fingers were still awkward with the buttons, but she was learning. *And I'll learn to do the housework, too,* she vowed, trying to comb her long auburn hair into some semblance of order. But the heavy hair was too much for her, and she dropped her hands weakly.

Hayley lifted her head, and looking again into the mirror, her eyes met Philip's. Their glances held for a long minute—they were alone in the house together for the first time. Hayley hastened to divert his attention.

"I'm sorry to be slow with everything. I wanted to arrange my hair and have supper on the table when you returned. I'm afraid I'm not much help at all."

Philip set the bucket of milk on the table and stood close behind her. Lifting a mass of the auburn hair, he reached for the brush she held. With long strokes he brushed her hair, and she luxuriated in the comfort of his skillful hands.

"Oh, that feels good. Paula worked with my hair on shipboard, but it hasn't had a good brushing since then." She leaned her cheek against his hand that was resting on her shoulder. "Thank you."

Philip dropped the brush on the chest and turned away abruptly. "Coil your hair, if you must, but I enjoy seeing it that way," he said huskily. A glance at his face accelerated Hayley's pulse. She took two combs from her satchel and pushed her hair away from her face with them, leaving the mass to hang freely over her shoulders. In England she might have been considered a woman of the street, but Philip didn't know that, and she owed him something.

Philip helped her place the food on the table, and they ate in silence. He volunteered to wash the utensils, but Hayley was adamant. "At least I can do that. You sit and rest; you've worked hard all day."

"Then, would you mind if I read from your Bible while you work?"

"Of course not." She brought the Bible from the dresser. "Consider the Bible yours to read whenever you want to."

Despite his interest in the Scripture, Philip lifted his head frequently to watch Hayley as she knelt in front of the hearth, clumsily and slowly washing bowls and spoons. She was perspiring from her efforts, but she smiled brightly at Philip when she came to sit opposite him at the table. "Would you read aloud?"

Philip rested the heavy Bible on the table. "Yes, it has always been a nightly custom at our house for Mum to read the Scriptures. I want it to be that way in my home, too. Do you have anything special you want to hear?"

"No, you choose."

Strange that Philip should choose to read from the book of Ruth, but as he read in carefully modulated tones, the words took on new meaning to Hayley. "Entreat me not to leave thee, or to return from following after thee: for whither thou goest, I will go; and where thou lodgest, I will lodge: thy people shall be my people, and thy God my God."

"You read well. Your mother taught you well."

"She has taught many native children to read the English words. Although she wonders often if her coming here as a missionary was an unfulfilled dream, I can see many good things she has accomplished."

He closed the Bible and smiled at Hayley. "I've always liked that Scripture, for it reminds me of my mother. The English preacher who married her to Father read those words."

"Why is it you bear her name, Lawrence, rather than that of your father, if they were married in the church?"

"The Algonquians don't use surnames as the English do; therefore, when I decided to live among the English, I had no other name to take. But it's a good name, and I like it. And, yes, Father and Mum were married by an English preacher. Although such a ceremony wasn't common among the natives, Mum insisted upon it."

The silence lengthened between them, until Philip said, "And now, Hayley, we must talk about . . . ," he hesitated, "our marriage. I knew you were ill that day in Jamestown, but I thought you were aware of our wedding ceremony, for you gave the answers distinctly, without hesitation. But since you didn't know what was happening, and obviously didn't come to the colony to be a bride, in all fairness, I don't think I should hold you to your vows."

"Do you want me to leave?" Hayley whispered, wondering why the idea didn't appeal to her.

"No, I don't want you to leave. But I don't want to hold you if you are unhappy."

"But if we took the vows in the church, how can we undo that?"

"I suppose as long as we haven't . . ." he paused, then smiled slightly, and his words brought warmth to Hayley's face. "As the Algonquians say, 'As long as I haven't covered you with my blanket,' we could mutually agree to dissolve the marriage."

Hayley refused to meet his eyes, and he continued, "Do you want to go to Jacques Guise?"

"No, I really don't. He is my mother's kinsman, but I'm not acquainted with him. Somehow he made me uncomfortable."

"So we agree on that. Can you tell me why you came to the colony?"

Remember your vow, she seemed to hear her uncle say. And after all, Philip was the nephew of the man who had caused Robert's death, and her father's and Roger's imprisonment.

"No, I can't tell you, except I was sent here by my family to be under the protection of Jacques Guise until I could return to England."

Toying with a spoon that was still lying on the table, Philip said, "You plan to return to England then?"

Thinking of what her life might be in England compared to staying here as Philip's wife, Hayley paused several minutes. "I'm not sure that I want to return to England, but I may have to. Women are not always allowed to choose their own destiny."

"But as my wife, according to English customs, wouldn't I be the one to make decisions for you?"

"I suppose so." Hayley's hands traced the outline of the Bible between them, and with eyes downcast, she murmured, "But if I stay, what do you expect of me?"

Philip came around the table and knelt by her side. He turned her face until their eyes met. "Hayley, for many years I have dreamed that some day I could share with some woman the great love my father and mother know. I had not thought that was possible. Someday I might have married a native woman because I would have wanted a family." He caressed her soft hair falling across his arm. "Already I feel the pull of my flesh to yours, but I cannot say I have the great love I know to be possible. In my heart I feel I will soon learn to love you. Tell me, have you ever known this great love for a man?"

His eyes wouldn't release her, and Hayley lowered her

63

lashes from his intense gaze, but Philip must have been aware of the pulse throbbing in her throat. She must answer truthfully, but she couldn't allow him to know too much of her life in England. His phrasing of the question, however, made it possible for her to answer honestly, "No, I have never experienced such a great love for any man."

"Look at me," he commanded, and Hayley seemed powerless to keep her eyes closed. His smile was beautiful. "Then perhaps you, too, could learn the great love for me?"

"Perhaps," Hayley answered, "if I have time." She could not tell him that the ambitions of her father and her uncle almost certainly would take her back to England, and soon. Of course, her need to see Little Roger tugged at her heart, too.

He pulled her close in a firm embrace and lowered his lips to hers. Although the caress was gentle, Hayley's composure was shaken. He released her.

"Then we will wait until the great love comes, as I'm sure it will." He smoothed the auburn hair back from her face. "Have you not brushed your own hair before now?"

"No, I've had servants," Hayley said, wondering if he would understand her previous lifestyle from that admission. "That's why I'm so useless here."

"You're far from useless to me," Philip assured her, "and I would consider it an honor to brush your hair. If I don't, I fear you will grow weary with it and cut it off, which would be such a pity," he added, as he drew the brush along her bright tresses.

Once her hair was brushed and gathered into a soft coil at the base of her neck, Philip reluctantly climbed the ladder to the loft. "Good-night, Hayley," he said softly when he put his foot on the bottom rung.

She held his glance and read there a promise that he was hers for the asking. But did she want him? She was tempted to call him to her side. As his wife, she would have a right to refuse to return to England, for the days of exile from her country had already convinced her of the futility of their effort to claim the throne. The title was doubtful at best, and she questioned their power to fight James I and his minions.

Her few days with Philip had given her no reason to doubt his strength and determination. If she assured him she wanted to stay with him, she was confident he would hold her against the power of her father and uncle. But she would lose her father, her uncle, and Roger. Was the freedom from political intrigue worth that?

And could she ever be happy here? In the light from the few glowing coals on the hearth, Hayley glanced around the room. Exchange the opportunity to become Queen of England, with all the majesty, power, and riches that entailed, for the few meager possessions in this hut? Denounce the right to rule for the toil of a colonial woman! Love for any man couldn't be worth all that, Hayley was sure. So she made no move to detain him, yet Philip's fervent caresses and gentleness were the last thing she remembered before sleep claimed her.

Their days developed a definite pattern. Philip would rise at dawn, kindle the fire, and awaken Hayley as he went through the room on his way to do the outside work. By the time he returned, she would have dressed and started to prepare the breakfast. After a few mornings of watching him, she had learned how to boil water for their tea and how to grind grain to be made into porridge.

After Philip left for the fields, Hayley spent the morning making her bed and washing the few utensils they'd used for breakfast. Once she climbed to the loft to see where Philip slept. The area was barren except for a mat of furs and coverlets. She was sleeping in his bed when he had nothing better than this, but she knew it would be useless to suggest that she sleep in the loft. Even without knowing her background, Philip often treated her as if she were a queen.

In the evening, Philip came in several hours before sunset to help Hayley prepare their supper. After the meal, Hayley tidied the room while Philip read to her from the Bible. When the house grew too dark for reading, he brushed her hair. Although he hadn't attempted to kiss her again, the tenderness of his hands and the way they lingered on her neck and forehead told her more than words would have, that already he was experiencing "the great love" for her.

When Maggie's provisions were all gone, Hayley tried to prepare the food, resulting in cut fingers and burned stew. Either she didn't keep enough water in the pots, or else the fire was blazing too high.

Hayley rubbed her forehead, deep in thought. How had the cornpone been made? Milk and eggs she remembered. Those she stirred together. Salt came next, a good-sized handful. She added cornmeal, and when stirred together, the batter resembled Maggie Lawrence's product. Noting by the sun's shadows that Philip would soon be in from the fields, she poured the batter into the three-legged skillet, put the lid on it, and shoved it under the coals in the fireplace.

Fidgeting with anticipation, Hayley hurriedly put the plates and bowls on the table. While Philip milked, she stirred the beans several times. No burned food tonight, and good cornbread, too. She hadn't tried to bake before, and she was eager for Philip to see what she had done.

When Philip seated himself at the table, Hayley brought the pot of beans, then hurried back to the fireplace for the bread. Placing her hand on the long handle to pull the bread from the ashes, she screamed.

Philip ran to her and lifted her right hand, where the imprint of the skillet handle showed plainly on her pale flesh. Without speaking, he reached for a jar of bear grease always handy on the mantle. He smeared the fat on the burn, which only intensified the pain, and Hayley had trouble holding back tears.

"Those iron handles hold heat. You always have to hold the handle with a cloth of some kind." He motioned to some furry mitts hanging beside the fireplace. "That's what those are for."

"I know, but I forgot. I was too eager to let you know I'd made bread for your supper." Philip's eyes held a tender expression as he wrapped a clean section of deerskin around her burn and led her to the table.

"You sit here, and I'll bring the bread. It isn't a bad burn, but you'll have to favor it for a few days."

When he carried the heavy skillet to the table, Hayley peered anxiously at the contents. Philip took a spoon and lifted a section of the bread, burned on top, yet underneath that hard crust, little changed from the consistency it had been when she put it in the pan.

Without any comment, Philip took a spoonful of the

bread on his plate and ate it. Hayley watched him anxiously. When he ate the whole section of bread and reached for more, Hayley brightened a bit. If he could eat seconds, it must not be too bad, so she held out her plate. After a slight hesitation, Philip gave her a small portion.

With her own spoon, Hayley took a bite of the bread. She gagged, and with difficulty, swallowed the distasteful food. Besides being unbaked, the bread was as salty as the water of the Atlantic.

Without looking at Philip, Hayley pushed back her plate, dropped her head on the table and wailed. Philip moved to sit beside her on the bench. Putting his arms around her, he drew the auburn head to his shoulder, and let her tears flow. He ran his fingers through the soft hair and massaged her neck and shoulders; slowly the tight muscles relaxed. "Hayley, I've told you before . . . you don't have to do this work."

"But I have to do something! Don't you realize how miserable I am all day here alone? I've never been by myself before. I must have something to do."

"But what did you do in England?"

"Sewed, read, played musical instruments, entertained the neighbors when they came to visit. Don't we have any neighbors? I haven't seen anyone except your father and mother since you brought me here." She raised her head and was surprised at the bitter look of frustration on his face.

"We have a few neighbors, but none are interested in being friendly with *me*. I'm half-English, but that half doesn't count with these people. All they can see is my Indian blood. But regardless, we don't live close enough in Virginia so you can see our neighbors often."

"But what about church? Surely there's a church we can attend. Sometimes I feel starved spiritually. I've always been taught that adversity is supposed to strengthen one's faith, but it isn't working that way with me. Worshiping with other people makes me stronger."

"There's a church at Wolstenholme Towne, besides the one at Jamestown. In fact, the colony has compulsory church attendance laws, but they don't seem to apply to me. You would be welcome, I suppose."

"Well, I won't go anyplace you aren't welcome."

Philip stood and stared into the dusk. "I'm sorry, Hayley, that I haven't been more considerate of you. I'm so busy trying to succeed in raising tobacco that I haven't thought of anything else. I just didn't realize what a drastic change you'd had in your life. Give me a few days, and I'll come up with something to make your life more pleasant."

The next day Hayley was even more restless. She fumbled around the house doing the few chores she could, but the bandaged hand made her more awkward than usual. The midday sun had turned the cabin into an oven, and Hayley paced the room until she could stand the heat no longer. Bolting outside to the edge of the slope, she saw Philip, near the river, walking through rows of tobacco well above his waist.

Suddenly seized with an inspiration, she rushed back into the house, found two small pieces of cake, all that was left of Maggie Lawrence's provisions, filled a jug with the morning's supply of goat's milk, and determinedly headed toward the field where Philip was working. Long before she reached him, she was panting from the unaccustomed exertion.

Hayley was standing beneath a tall pine tree when Philip looked up and saw her. She waved shyly at him, and he caught his breath. Because she was so thin and without color when she'd first arrived, Philip hadn't realized what a beautiful woman he'd married. Standing now, straight and tall, with color in her face from the long walk, the sun filtering through the pine tree on her auburn hair, she was a vision of beauty. Philip's emotions raced when he realized that this beautiful woman was his. He forced himself to walk deliberately toward her, removing suckers from the tobacco plants as he walked. "Good morning," he called, and willed his voiced to its normal pitch.

"I brought you something. Are you so busy that you can't stop to eat the last of your mother's cake?"

Wiping his sticky hands on the side of his trousers, he took her hand and led her into the heavier shade of an oak tree. "Never too busy for your company, milady, food or not."

Philip lounged on the ground, and Hayley sat beside him, as they leisurely ate the food.

"You work too hard, Philip. Can't you find anyone to help you?"

"I'd like to hire an indentured servant, but I don't have enough money to do that."

"I don't understand."

"They're people who come from England and hire themselves to a planter, who will pay their boat passage in return for the servant's work over a period of five to seven years."

"Does it cost so much to hire one?"

"Not a great deal, but for someone like me, who had

nothing except land to start with, money is scarce. If this crop of tobacco is a good one, I should be able to hire a servant."

"You used your tobacco to pay my fare to America! But Philip, my way was already paid. My uncle paid the captain . . . you know I didn't come over like the rest of the women. Can't you have your money returned?"

"I doubt it. By now the *Jonathan* has returned to England, and who would believe *me?* It isn't your fault, and you're worth more than an indentured servant to me," he said daringly.

Glancing down at her bandaged hand, Hayley replied, "I doubt that. You have to work in the field and then work at the house, too. I haven't brought you anything but trouble."

Philip protested, and if she'd looked at him then, she would have known the fullness of his heart, for he looked at her with that special tenderness a man holds for only one woman. But Hayley's mind was on something else.

"You know that I have a bag of coins. Please use those, and hire someone to help you."

"I won't do that," Philip asserted. "You must have had some reason for bringing those coins."

"To pay my return fare to England, but I may never be allowed to go back anyway."

"Hayley, I've been thinking about our talk last night. If you really want to learn to do the housework, I'll take you to my mother, and she will teach you what to do."

"She would have taught me when she was here, but I was ashamed to admit I knew so little."

He laughed and tugged playfully on a tendril of hair that

had escaped from the roll at the back of her neck. "Don't you suppose she suspected that? Remember she had to adjust to a new way of living over here. In a few days I'll have the tobacco fields so that I can leave, and I'll take you to their home. I won't ask her to leave Father again."

Philip lay back with his hands under his head, and Hayley ran her fingers idly over the muscles that bulged through his fustian shirt.

"And after you come back from Mum's," Philip continued, trying to ignore the sensations her hands were kindling, "I'll take you into Jamestown for a visit. You can see Paula. I've decided I'm going to forget that my Indian blood has made me inferior in the sight of others. Many people have triumphed over similar burdens. I'm going to become a part of the life in Jamestown, make myself so pleasant that people will forget I'm part Indian. They occasionally have social functions, and we'll attend those."

"I didn't mean to be a baby about what I'd left behind. I was remembering only the good things . . . life wasn't all good in England."

Philip waited for Hayley to explain, but when she said no more, his eyes swept the long valley before him and the broad James as it flowed relentlessly toward the sea.

"I've big dreams for this place, Hayley. When I look around now, I see more than a crude hut on a hill and a few fields of tobacco and grain. I see a large house like my mother's home in England, and ladies and gentlemen in rich dress strolling around a formal lawn and garden. I see important people coming to Haywood because it's a social center in Virginia."

"Haywood! You didn't tell me you had a name for your plantation."

"I hadn't one until you came."

"It's a beautiful name, and I like it. But, Philip, I was reading in the Bible this morning from Psalm 127, where it says, 'Except the Lord build the house, they labour in vain that build it.' Don't leave *him* out of your plans."

"No, I won't. Mum has taught me too well for me to forsake my Lord. When I first came to this spot and wanted it for my own, I knelt under this very tree and prayed. I promised the Lord then, just like Joshua of old had done, 'As for me and my house, we will serve the Lord.'"

"If you have that resolve, Philip, nothing can stop you from attaining your dreams."

"We may not live to see that attainment, but our children will. I'm going to leave them a strong heritage."

"*Our* children?"

He rolled toward her and pulled her down beside him on the grass. "Our children! You're mine, Hayley. I feel it in my heart. I won't force you into a marriage relationship, but I know one day it will be so. Tell me, my dearest, that you share the same longing that I do."

His lips were persuasive, his hands eager, and Hayley reveled in the ecstasy of a mature woman. He knew she was on the point of yielding to him, and his pulse leaped exaltingly. But her body suddenly wilted, and she pulled away from his insistent arms. The memory of Roger had come between them.

"Until I hear from my family in England, I can tell you nothing."

chapter

5

ALTHOUGH THE LATE JULY MIDMORNING SUN was shining brightly, in places the foliage was so heavy that no rays penetrated to the forest floor. Hayley's feet burned in the deerhide moccasins Philip had made her, and pains shot through her hips from the unaccustomed walking. They had been climbing gradually for what seemed hours, and Hayley wondered how much farther she could walk.

At last Philip stopped. "Would you like to rest?"

"Oh, yes, please. I've never walked such a long way before."

Philip said contritely, "I should have thought of that. Why didn't you tell me? Still trying to prove you're capable of being a Virginia colonist, I suppose?"

His smile told her he was teasing her, but she flushed anyway and didn't respond. Philip pointed ahead to a flat rock beside the trail.

"We can sit there to rest, for we have plenty of time to arrive at Mum's, and then for me to return to the plantation before dark."

Although the rock was hard, Hayley was relieved to sit down. She pulled off the moccasins and stretched her feet.

Rubbing her ankles, she asked, "How long must I stay at your mother's to learn what I need to know?" Although she had enjoyed the companionship of Maggie Lawrence, she wasn't looking forward to being left alone with her and Towaye, for they still seemed like strangers to her.

"Just a few days, I think, but I probably won't come back for a week."

"Why can't you stay?"

"I have goats and chickens to care for, and I don't like to stay away from the plantation very long."

"Surely you could stay overnight. This walk is too long for twice in one day."

"It isn't long for me. This is easier work than in the tobacco fields." He looked keenly at her. "You know, of course, if I stay overnight, Mum will expect us to share a bed. And I wish you wouldn't say anything about our private lives. Mum will be upset enough if you someday return to England. No need to concern her about it now."

His parents' house was even smaller than Philip's, but the furnishings were much the same. When Maggie Lawrence learned why they'd come, she threw her arms around Hayley. "Of course I'll teach you to cook. It really isn't such a hard task, for we don't have a great variety of foods. I'll enjoy doing it."

She set out some food for Philip before his return. While they sat at the table, Hayley felt a chill of fear, as real as if cold water had drenched her body. She turned quickly. A young Indian stood in the doorway, his dark eyes piercing and hostile. She gasped and looked away quickly when she met his venomous stare. Philip glanced up to see what had disturbed her.

"Greetings, Saponi," Philip said, but the other man didn't return the salutation.

"Come in, son," Maggie Lawrence said. "Philip is leaving soon, and he's eating a bite now. Will you join us?"

Saponi appeared to be younger than Philip, and he shared none of his brother's good looks. He was slight of build and walked with a limping gait. Standing beside the fireplace, with one foot on a bench, he sullenly answered his mother, but Hayley didn't understand a word he said, for he spoke in Algonquian.

"Hayley, this is my younger son, Saponi; this is Philip's wife." Saponi acknowledged her presence with a curt nod, but his eyes boldly assessed her person.

Listening in silence to the strange conversation, Hayley marveled at the difference between Saponi and the rest of his family. Philip and Maggie spoke in English, and whenever Saponi bothered to speak at all, he muttered in Algonquian. She had gathered from Philip that his brother was not often at home, but wandered the forest most of the time, and Hayley fervently wished he hadn't chosen to be present during her visit.

Time for Philip's departure came all too soon for Hayley, and he drew her out into the yard with him. Pulling her close to him with one arm, he whispered, "If I'd known he would be at home, I wouldn't have brought you. Your stay may not be pleasant."

"But can't he speak English?"

"As well as I, but he refuses to do so. A few years ago, he decided to renounce English ways completely, and as the settlers have arrived in greater numbers, he has grown even more bitter. I don't think he will bother you, but stay close to Mum or Father all the time. Don't leave the house by yourself."

"You make me afraid."

He traced the curve of her face with his forefinger, and rested it gently on her lips. "I don't think you need to be, but I want you to be cautious. I'm going to miss you, Hayley."

"I'm going to miss you, too," she replied and knew that it was the truth. In such a short time, she'd grown accustomed to his company; she didn't want to leave him at all. *And what will you do when you are summoned back to England, if you aren't content for a few days' separation?* she asked herself.

He bent to kiss her forehead, and her arms encircled his waist as she clung to him. "I'll return for you soon," he whispered.

As he led her back toward the house, Hayley noted that Saponi stood in the doorway watching their farewell.

"Take care of her for me, Mum." Hayley stood by the door and watched until he was out of sight. Just before he disappeared into the forest, he turned to wave, and Hayley's eyes moistened with loneliness.

Saponi seemed in no notion of leaving, and every move she made, Hayley felt his eyes upon her. "Son," his mother asked at bedtime, "are you staying the night?"

She answered his Algonquian, "Very well, you may sleep in the loft. Hayley, we'll spread a mat for you here beside our bed."

What might I fear from Saponi? she wondered. Even after he had climbed the ladder to the loft, and after his parents had gone to bed, Hayley lay awake, listening. If Saponi hated the English as they had indicated, her life might be endangered, but Hayley suspected more than that. She had once observed lust in the eyes of her father's coachman, Arnold Wright. Hadn't Saponi exhibited the same emotion when he looked at her?

Remembering Wright caused Hayley to wonder why he had been spying on the *Jonathan* the day she left England. He had no reason to feel kindly toward Hayley, and even now, she remembered the repulsion of years ago when she had rebuffed his advances toward her.

Hearing the couple's affectionate murmurs, Hayley turned uncomfortably on her mat. When the murmuring turned to the gentle breathing of their sleep, Hayley wondered, *Can I stand a week of this?* The situation reminded her of the close quarters on the *Jonathan,* when she had been surrounded by ninety women. She thought she'd grown used to sleeping on the floor during that ocean voyage, but she found she was still uncomfortable.

Saponi didn't stay in the house all of the time, and without his disturbing presence, Hayley rapidly learned the things that her mother-in-law had to tell her. Each evening she went with the older woman to the goat pen, and in a few days, she was able to extract a bit of milk from the goat's udder.

"I'm pleased you're willing to learn our way of life. It is hard for you, but it's the only way the English will survive here. Eventually we might have a life of ease such as we knew at home, but not for a long time."

The visit was marred by one unpleasant experience during a short space of time when Hayley was alone in the house, peeling carrots by the fireplace. Suddenly, although she hadn't heard a sound, she sensed a presence behind her. Saponi! He stood so close that Hayley moved her stool away from him.

"Why do not all the English women look the same as do our women? I thought all English women had the golden hair as my mother, but your head is crowned with the color of the oak leaves in the waning of the year." He lifted a long tendril of her hair that had escaped the twist she had made at the back of her head.

Hayley feared his touch, but she said nothing. Philip was right; Saponi could speak English when he wanted to.

"Again my brother has beaten me. He was the firstborn. He was given the tall frame, the body free from scars. And now he has first gotten the woman that I want to possess."

Hayley stood abruptly, and the bowl of vegetables scattered at her feet. "Please don't talk that way," she said. "How could you want me? Until a few days ago, you hadn't seen me at all."

He reached out to touch her face, and Hayley brushed his hand away.

"I know in a glance what I want. You will be mine."

Hearing a sound at the door, Hayley turned in relief to see Towaye's tall frame in the doorway. Speaking in angry Algonquian, Towaye admonished his son. Saponi answered his father in bitter tones and spinning on his heel with a noticeable limp, he left the house.

"Are you all right, my child?"

"Oh, yes. Please don't tell your wife," Hayley begged, and dropping to her knees, hurriedly picked up the scattered vegetables.

Hayley tried to put the unpleasant incident from her

mind, for Saponi didn't return that evening, and she could concentrate on her cooking instructions. She was pleased with her progress and was becoming eager to return to Philip's home to put some of her newly learned skills into practice.

Six days had passed since Philip had brought her to his parents' home, and Hayley looked out the door hoping to see him returning. She didn't see Philip, but Saponi was walking toward the house, and behind him sauntered an Indian girl. Straight black hair hung over lavishly decorated buckskin garments, and with her olive skin and dark brown eyes, the girl's appearance was commanding, rather than beautiful.

Maggie Lawrence didn't see them until they walked into the house, and when she turned, she dropped the wooden bowl she was cleansing.

"Nonna!" she exclaimed. Going swiftly to the girl, she greeted her in Algonquian. Explaining to Hayley, she said, "This is Nonna, daughter of Chief Opechancanough. She is . . . our friend."

Will Philip never get here? Hayley thought in panic. Another Indian was more than she could cope with today. Nonna squatted beside the fire and helped herself to a bowl of beans. Saponi took a bowl that his mother handed to him and stooped beside the fireplace to eat. Hayley tried to avoid his gaze, which seemed to follow her every move.

Hayley sensed an uncomfortable situation, but since she couldn't understand a word of their conversation, she didn't know the reasons. Glancing out the door for what must have been the fiftieth time that day, she spotted Philip and Towaye walking toward the house. With a glad cry she ran from the building; Philip held out his arms, and she sought their shelter.

"How's my colonial lady?" He smiled down at her.

"I know enough to go home now." Home! Had it really become home to her? "I'm ready to leave."

Towaye muttered something in Algonquian, and Philip looked toward the house. Nonna was standing in the door, and Hayley sensed the tension that ran through her husband's body.

Nonna retreated into the room when they reached the door. Allowing Hayley to precede him into the house, Philip hugged his mother and kissed her on the cheek. Then angrily, or so it seemed to Hayley, he turned to Saponi.

Hayley was a silent spectator to the scene between the two brothers. For at least ten minutes, Philip and Saponi spoke heatedly, with Saponi gesturing wildly toward Hayley, and then to Nonna, who frequently entered the conversation. The confrontation ended when Saponi grabbed Nonna by the arm, and with the girl in tow, rushed from the house. Towaye's expressionless face hid his thoughts, but distress was written widely across his wife's visage.

When the two had gone, Philip addressed his father, still speaking in Algonquian, and Towaye threw wide his arms in a gesture of bewilderment.

"Mum," Philip said, speaking in English. "Could you spare a bowl of beans? I want to start back right away. I hear you've turned my wife into a skilled colonial now."

"She has learned rapidly, but you should still help her awhile." She dished up food for all of them. When she placed chunks of cornbread on the table, Hayley breathed a sigh of relief. She had made the bread, and she prided herself that it tasted and looked as good as Maggie Lawrence's own.

Despite the unpleasantness of Saponi's presence, Hayley had enjoyed the week, and she said good-by with some regret. The return trip was not as strenuous as the earlier walk because they traveled downhill most of the way.

During their rest stop, and while they nibbled on dried meat and grain, Hayley asked, "What were you and Saponi arguing about this morning?"

"I'm not sure I should tell you."

"Why not? I thought the conversation concerned me."

"Nonna and I have been . . . " he hesitated, "friends. If you hadn't come into my life, I might have taken her for my woman; mating customs are not the same among the Indians as the English. Saponi was demanding today that I choose between you and Nonna."

So he could have me for himself, I suppose, Hayley thought, but she said aloud, "And you chose me?"

"I chose you," he said simply. "When he left, he angrily said that he would take Nonna for his own woman. Now that doesn't bother me as far as Nonna is concerned, but I don't like to see Saponi allied so closely with Nonna's father, Opechancanough. I fear for the English community because of Opechancanough's hatred of them, and it would be a great sadness to my parents if Saponi should be involved in such trouble. No doubt he will capitalize on my rejection of Nonna to further alienate Saponi against the English."

"I'm afraid of Saponi," Hayley said, and Philip took her hand.

"Why? Tell me," he demanded, but she shook her head. Already too much ill will separated the two brothers, and she refused to be the cause of more.

"I will protect you from any danger," Philip promised. "From now on, I don't expect to be very far away from you. I have missed you, my dearest one."

As they continued their journey, Hayley's thoughts went to Philip's admission that Nonna had been his friend. *How good a friend?* She knew she dared not ask. With all the secrets surrounding her past, Philip was surely entitled to a few of his own.

chapter

6

A WAVE OF COOL AIR SWEPT IN from the James, and Hayley closed the door to retain the fireplace heat. Philip would be late tonight, for he hoped to finish cutting the tobacco before the day's end. With deftness she gathered the eggs, fed the chickens, and proceeded to the pen where the goats were housed. In a short time, she had the bucket half-full of milk. Philip praised her work often, and she knew his approval was deserved. In the six weeks since they'd returned, she had become an efficient housewife. No longer did time hang heavy upon her hands; always some task was to be performed.

At times, Hayley looked at her work-scarred hands and shuddered, remembering when the most work she did in a day's time was simple embroidery. And although she often went to bed with a sore and weary body, would she ever be content to return to that life of leisure? Considering the many months that had elapsed since her escape from England, she often wondered why she had no word from her uncle. Had he, too, been imprisoned? Little by little, Hayley's life in England had become less important to her, yet she longed to know the fate of her loved ones.

In those weeks also, Philip and Hayley had become friends. She often walked to the fields for a midday visit or went late in the afternoon to walk home with him. Whatever Philip's physical feelings toward her, he was suppressing them and seemed content to allow Hayley time to make her own decision about their relationship. But Hayley realized they couldn't continue indefinitely as they were.

Philip's lingering fingers on her shoulders and arms when he brushed her hair each night generated a longing in Hayley that she suppressed with difficulty. More than once, she had almost called him back when his reluctant steps approached the ladder. And once he had dropped his lips to her shoulders in a caress so unnerving that Hayley couldn't sleep at all that night, while above her, in the loft, she heard Philip turning often in his own bed.

After taking the milk into the house, Hayley checked the fire and the vegetables she was preparing for supper. Everything was in order, and she would have time to walk to the field. She knew that completing the tobacco harvest was important to Philip, and she wanted to share it with him. Throwing a gray shawl over her russet dress, she left the house.

The walk to the tobacco field was no longer tiring to her. Walking firmly, head and shoulders thrown back, she became aware of the pungent scent of the tobacco mixed with the tang of the James. Passing the field of ripening corn, she knew that as soon as the tobacco was harvested, the corn must be cut and shucked before winter.

Only a few stalks of tobacco were still standing, and unobserved, Hayley watched Philip swing the sharp knife and bring them to the ground. He deftly split the stalks and slipped them over a sharpened stick, which was then pushed into the ground to give the tobacco another day to dry in the sun before being hung in the pole barn along with other stalks already harvested.

Hayley's approving applause brought a smile to his features, and when he walked toward her, Hayley's body and spirit reached out to him with a magnetic thrill. This man had woven himself into her heart. His shirt and breeches were soiled from working; his hands, sticky from tobacco leaves, but her pulse trembled at the sight of him.

"I'm too dirty to touch you, but I want to, Hayley. How I long for you! I've worked beyond my physical capacity today, and for the past hour, I was wondering, 'Is it worth all this hard work?' Then I look up and see you standing here, the weariness flees, and my ambition returns. What a difference you've made in my life!"

"Then you're not sorry I'm here instead of Nonna?" Hayley hated herself for even asking the question, for she'd been careful not to mention the girl's name since their return.

Irritation flitted across Philip's face, and the romantic moment was gone. "I have told you Nonna is a part of my past. She should not be named between us again. I chose you."

In spite of the fact that she had obviously annoyed him, Philip continued, "Come with me while I unload the tobacco sticks, and we'll walk home together." Wordlessly, feeling much like a reprimanded child, she followed him as he led the ox to the tobacco barn, where he climbed the ladder to hang a stick laden with tobacco on a high pole rafter. As he clambered back down the ladder, Hayley said, "Why can't I hand them up to you, so you won't have to come down each time?"

"Your dress will be soiled."

Without comment, Hayley lifted a stick of tobacco and handed it to him. It wasn't an easy task, for the tobacco was heavier than she had thought, nor did she like the sticky substance that adhered to her hands and clothes. But she was helping Philip, and nothing else mattered.

Hayley leaned on the fence while Philip removed the heavy yoke from the ox and threw grain for him to eat.

"King James doesn't like tobacco. Although he's forbidden its use, still the custom of smoking the leaves has spread in England. He calls it a stinking weed and says it is harmful to the nose, the head, and the lungs."

"I agree with King James," Philip said, "but if it hadn't been for tobacco, the colony named for him would have disappeared long ago. The settlers have tried many projects to make money for the London Company, but nothing has been profitable except raising tobacco. For the first time, the company is getting some return on its investment."

As they started up the hill toward the house, he continued, "The Indians primarily use tobacco for ritualistic purposes, and even for medicine. They aren't addicted to its use like the English and Spanish."

"So much the better for them, I'm sure."

Later, when Philip was brushing her hair for the night, he said, "Tomorrow I will hang the rest of the tobacco in the barn, and I can leave for a few days. Would you like to go into Jamestown? If we leave Saturday, you could probably stay overnight with your friend, Paula, and then go to church on Sunday."

She clutched his arm so quickly that he dropped the hair brush. "Oh, Philip, please. But I'm not going to the church without you. I'm sure you will be welcomed. I'd like to see another English woman, but I want to go to church, too. I pray and read the Bible alone, but I have a desire to worship with others."

All the next day, Hayley was busy with preparations for the journey. She washed all their clothing, and chose the best of her garments to take for church on Sunday, shaking her head sadly as she compared the *best* she had now to the garments she had left behind in England.

She was even more distressed over Philip's clothes—he had such a few garments, most of them worn. She lifted the bag of coins that had lain in the chest for weeks and took two sovereigns from the leather bag to place in her satchel. She decided the bottom of the grain barrel was a safe hiding place and put the rest of the coins there. Money was too scarce in the colony to be careless.

Philip apparently sympathized with her excitement over the journey, for Hayley suspected that he realized by now that his marriage to her in the Jamestown church had plunged her into an existence that was far inferior to what she'd known in England.

"How will we travel, Philip?"

"We'll walk, if you think you are up to it. By walking, we can cut across country through the forest, but with the ox cart, we would need to stay near the level land beside the river. Walking will be the quickest way to travel."

"Oh, I'm used to walking now, but will we be able to take a change of clothing if we walk?"

"Surely, but don't try to take the satchel." He went to the loft and returned with two buckskin packs. One was already filled, as though Philip had made his own preparations for the journey.

"I can carry your pack as well as mine, if you'll place your belongings inside."

"What are you taking?"

Philip unrolled the pack to show Hayley the most beautiful furs she'd ever seen. "These are mink and marten hides. I trapped them last winter, and I may want to do some trading in Jamestown. These should be worth quite a lot in barter."

"But what do they have for trade?"

"I always trade for spices, sugar, and other items that Mum uses for cooking. Occasionally a boat will bring more products from England, but their cost is high."

"Philip, is it possible to buy materials for clothing? You could use some new breeches, shirts, doublets. If you're going to become a proper English gentleman, you need some better clothing."

"We can see what is available, but the garments would have to be made. Are you handy with a needle?"

She shook her head sadly. "Not the way you mean. I don't know how to make a garment."

"Perhaps some of the women who came with you on the *Jonathan* are seamstresses."

Even in his old clothing, Hayley was pleased with Philip's appearance when they started toward Jamestown. Brown woven stockings met his heavy tan breeches at the knees. The linen shirt of blue seemed to reflect the color of his eyes, and when he put on a new fringed deerskin coat, her eyes glowed with pride. "I'll be proud to be seen with you, husband," she said, and the light in his eyes reminded her how much he longed for acceptance.

The cross-country walk to Jamestown took almost half a day because of hills to climb and swampy areas to avoid. But when they left the forest and started across the clearing to the fort, the area was as welcome to Hayley as a sight of London after weeks of exile in Devonshire.

A strong palisade and fort stood near the banks of the James, and behind it and to the side, several rows of houses had been constructed. Rough clapboard houses, some two-storied, were beginning to replace the daub and wattle structures built by the first settlers.

Short wooden fences surrounded many of the houses, and the influence of the brides could be seen in the late-blooming flowers near the homes, as well as by the dainty curtains that stirred around open windows. Women and men walked together along a main street, where three colorful tents protected tables of merchandise. Hayley peered with interest at the items for sale, but Philip, intent on finding a lodging place for his wife, hurried on by the market.

Only a few inquiries were needed to find Paula, for Walter, the potter, was well-known. Their house, a simple one-room clapboard dwelling built on a brick foundation, was two streets from the James.

Paula stared in disbelief when she opened the door.

"Gracious! I've wondered over and over what happened to you. Come in." Hayley entered the house, but when Philip hesitated on the doorstep, Paula took his arm. "Come on in, so we can close the door. The wind off the James is cutting today."

Philip's height seemed to shrink the little cottage when he diffidently stepped inside. He had never been invited into a Jamestown home before.

"After you placed her into my care that day, I paid Hayley's fare, married her, and took her to my plantation east of here."

"You were so ill, I wondered if you'd ever recover, but I can see that your health has returned. Being married has certainly agreed with you. You look like you did that day when you boarded the *Jonathan* in England."

Hayley glanced quickly at Philip, and she felt her face growing warm. "I can return the compliment. You look wonderful, Paula." The blond woman was even plumper than usual, and Hayley suspected that she was in the early months of pregnancy.

"Would it be possible for Hayley to spend the night here with you?" Philip asked. "We want to stay for church services tomorrow. I have some trading to do this afternoon, but I need to find a place for her to sleep."

"Of course she can stay here," Paula cried, and Hayley couldn't doubt her welcome. "You come back in time for supper, and you and Walter can sleep in the loft. Hayley can share my bed."

Philip demurred at the invitation. "You can probably tell by looking at me that I'm of mixed blood. Your husband may not welcome me as you do."

Paula waved that aside. "I've heard Walter say more than once that the only salvation for the English in this country is to learn to live with the natives instead of fighting them. You are welcome here."

As soon as Philip left, Hayley hastily said, "Is there any

place in Jamestown where materials for men's clothing may be obtained? Philip's garments are almost threadbare."

"A ship came in from London last week loaded with bolts of broadcloth and fustian, but enough for a man's garments would cost over three shillings, so not many people were buying. I fingered it and wished for enough to make some clothes for Walter, but no use. Money is scarce in Jamestown." She paused, and her eyes lighted expressively. "And, Hayley, the most gorgeous silks and velvets. Beautiful. It's terrible to be poor, isn't it?"

How could Hayley answer? She'd never known poverty until these months of deprivation she'd shared with Philip.

"Not that I'm complaining," Paula continued, "for we have so much more here in America than we could ever have hoped for in England . . . Walter working at his own craft and making a living for us. We may be poor now, but we don't expect to be always."

Unable to understand the changes in the Johnsons' lives, Hayley didn't reply, but asked instead, "Do you know of anyone who can do sewing?"

"Oh, yes, several fine seamstresses came over with the Ninety. And I do a bit of fine work meself, if I do say so. I've earned a few shillings sewing for the Jamestown bachelors."

"I have two sovereigns that I want to use to buy some material. If you'll make a set of clothes for Philip, we will also buy enough for an outfit for Walter. That can be the pay for your work."

"Wonderful! Let's go bargain with the merchant now. You let me do the talking." Grabbing Hayley's hand, Paula hurried out of the house and down the grassy street.

The merchant reminded Hayley of those she'd seen on market days at home, and she and Paula laughed at his efforts to outwit them. But his eyes gleamed at the sovereigns, and Hayley knew he didn't often have the opportunity to swap his merchandise for gold.

After a lot of good-natured haggling, in exchange for the sovereigns, they carried away enough broadcloth for four shirts, blue linen for doublet facing, fustian yardage for two pairs of breeches, and a length of leather for a pair of breeches for Philip. Paula also bargained for enough buttons and thread to make the items.

"I've needles of me own, but me shears are not worthy to cut such fine materials." So the merchant added a set of shears and two sets of bone combs to their purchases.

Hayley ran her hands over the silk materials, wishing she had brought another gold sovereign. So many days had passed since she had worn her regal garments, but what good would a silk dress be on the plantation? No doubt the remainder of the coins would serve a better purpose than to dress her in silk.

Walter returned to the house before Philip arrived, and Hayley watched closely; his greeting to Philip contained no intimidation and although he must have been aware of Philip's mixed heritage, he gave no sign. When they sat at the table, and Walter bowed his head over the food, Hayley breathed a word of thanks on her own—thanks that Philip was welcomed. Surely his marriage to her would encourage other people to accept him.

Hayley liked Walter's cheerful outlook on the affairs of the colony. His brown eyes glistened as he pushed dark brown hair from his forehead and directed a question to

Philip. "As a native here, what do you think of Jamestown's chance of survival?"

Hesitantly, Philip answered, "If they can avoid trouble with the natives, the English can prosper. However, if my information is correct, I believe the London Company has placed impossible demands on the settlers. No gold is here for them to find, nor a passage from here to a great ocean to the west. Not many days' journey away, the mountains are rugged, with no water passage."

"You strike me right, mate. That's the first sensible answer I've had from anyone here. If we want to make our homes in this country, it can be done by hard work, but no one is going to get rich any other way."

When they finished the meal, Philip said to Paula, "Do you know of a seamstress in the village?"

Hayley glanced quickly at Paula, who, with a wink, laughed and said, "Quite a few, and I'm one of them. In England, I was a great lady's maid, and I made all her garments. Why do you ask?"

Rising from the table, Philip brought his deerhide pack from the step. Hayley gasped when he unwrapped it. Three bolts of silk material gleamed in the candlelight. "I thought this green color would bring out those flecks in your eyes, Hayley, and I wanted Mum to have a dress of the blue yardage. I know she has often longed for the kind of gowns she wore in England. And this length is for you, Paula, if you'll make the other garments." He held out a piece of deep rose silk that would compliment Paula's blond features.

"But, Philip, you needed clothes worse than I. What did you buy for yourself?"

"Only some heavy leather for shoes. I'll make them this winter. I bargained hard, but my furs didn't stretch far enough for anything else."

Paula regarded Hayley, a question in her eyes, and at Hayley's nod, she went to the corner where she'd hidden their afternoon purchases. Spreading them out on the table before Philip and Walter, she said, "Hayley had a similar idea, Philip. She used gold sovereigns to buy some material for your garments. In return for my making them, Walter will have some new clothes."

Walter lifted a piece of the broadcloth and holding it over his shoulder, said, "We'll be dressed like dandies, won't we? Next time you come to Jamestown, we'll be the best-dressed people here. Maybe we can throw a party."

Long after the men sought their pallets in the loft, Paula and Hayley spread the shimmering material on the bed and discussed ways to fashion it.

With the thought that she'd soon have a new green silk gown, Hayley didn't mind the russet homespun she wore to church the next morning. She walked happily with Philip at her side to the wooden structure erected outside the fort on a cobblestone foundation.

Philip entered the building hesitantly, but no one asked him to leave, and he sat on a wooden bench beside Hayley and the Johnsons.

Seeing the crude pulpit and rustic wooden cross before her, Hayley remembered the last time she'd worshiped in England at the huge cathedral near her home. No high vaulted nave here, no stained glass windows, no statues. Hand-carved products of the New World had been used for this sanctuary, but as Hayley joined in the ritual and the reciting of Psalms, she was renewed in her soul.

Is this the church where Philip and I were married? As if he read her thoughts, Philip nodded his head.

The minister remembered them, and he shook her hand. "Mistress Lawrence, you look much improved in health since the last time you were here."

"Yes, my husband and his family cared for me. I've been quite happy here in the colony," Hayley told him, suddenly realizing the truth of the words.

The trip home from Jamestown was a pleasant one, and Hayley hardly noticed the many miles as they talked about their visit. For those two days she'd been able to put aside the worry about her father and Roger—for a few hours she had ceased to wonder if they were still alive, and if Robert had really been killed. *What if he were still alive?*

Hayley was as pleased at the change in Philip as she was in her own feelings. How much it had meant to him to be invited into a Jamestown home, to sit down in worship with the English, and to be served communion!

"Walter Johnson is a fine man, and he's going to be important to the colony someday. And I am, too, Hayley. I'm going to make a place for the Lawrence family in Virginia. Walter even suggested that I stand for election to the House of Burgesses from my district next spring. I'm going to think about it."

Towaye was sitting on the step when they arrived at the house.

"Father! Is everything all right? Did Mum come with you?"

"Your mother is fine. I didn't know you were away, and I came with some news. I was about to give up and return home."

"The news . . . is it good or bad?"

"That I do not know," Towaye said as he followed them inside. Philip laid aside his pack and started the fire while Towaye talked.

"A runner came to our house yesterday with an invitation from Opechancanough to attend the harvest festival at his village. Saponi is going to cover Nonna with his blanket during the festival."

Philip's hands halted momentarily at his task, and he shot a piercing glance at his father. "Well, can that be bad? He'd threatened to do that."

"It's not that Saponi is taking a woman. I don't like this invitation from Opechancanough. Trouble is coming, Philip, and for my Maggie's sake, I want to avoid it."

"You think he's trying to make us take a stand for or against the settlers?"

"Yes, for he sent word that you should come also."

"I've already made my choice, Father. You know that." Philip's glance traveled to Hayley, who had been removing her cape and placing her belongings on the chest.

"But it isn't that easy for your mother and me. We have two sons."

Philip laid his arms around Towaye's shoulders, which seemed more stooped than the last time Hayley had seen him.

"Father, I'm sorry I've caused you any grief because my brother and I cannot agree."

Towaye shook his head. "The fault is not yours, my son.

If anyone is at fault, it would be your mother and me, who've given you mixed blood. But our love was so strong, we didn't consider what the future might hold for our offspring."

"I will go to the festival and see what he has to say." Drawing Hayley toward him, Philip continued, "But what about Hayley? Should I take her?"

"My Maggie will go with me," Towaye answered, but the expressive shrug of his shoulders left their decision up to them.

"I don't understand what the problem is," Hayley said. "Do you expect trouble if you go to this festival?"

"I don't know," Philip told her. "Although most of the English think the natives are peaceful, we believe trouble is coming, and Opechancanough is trying to involve us. Trouble is unlikely at the village, but you must make the decision. The journey will be rough, and if you don't want to come along, I'm sure Paula will welcome you."

Hayley thought of the last time she'd seen Robert, Roger, and her father with no hint that she might never see them again. She couldn't tolerate the thought of losing another person she loved. Her heart skipped a beat when that thought entered her mind. *Lose another person I love!* Had it come to that? Did she love this man?

"I'm going with you. Anything is better than wondering, not knowing what has happened to you. I've experienced that before."

Philip's eyes lighted at this admission, and he squeezed her shoulders tightly.

"We should leave day after tomorrow," Towaye said. "Now I must return to your mother."

chapter

7

THE JOURNEY PROVED TO BE MORE STRENUOUS than Hayley had imagined. The trail was rough and upward, and Towaye, walking in front, set a steady pace. Maggie had provided Hayley with a buckskin garment, which hung about six inches below her knees, giving her more mobility than her long dress would have. She wore a cape, but in spite of their rapid walking, she was cool.

They traveled through thick woodlands. Hayley had thought the beauty of spring and summer in the colony was beyond equal, but the variety of hues on the maple and oak trees was breathtaking, reminding her of the season in England. Because the four of them did little talking during the day, Hayley spent much of the time thinking about her childhood. She tried to avoid the thought that they would soon be in the village of Opechancanough, a man with an avowed hatred of the English. She was English. How would he react to her presence?

When they stopped for the night, Philip spread a bearskin on the ground for her bed, and she rolled up in it, but the coolness of the earth still seeped into her body. Philip lay near her, and when she awakened several times, cold and uncomfortable, she looked enviously at Towaye and his wife, who shared their warmth wrapped together in one skin.

They reached Opechancanough's town in late afternoon, and Saponi and Nonna came to greet them. Randomly located bark huts covered a larger area than Hayley had imagined, and cooking fires in the center of the village were crowded with steaming pots. A few lean dogs yapped at their approach, and a bevy of wide-eyed brown children stared at them. Philip's youth must have been spent in just this kind of environment.

Hayley couldn't determine how many people were in the village, but they were numerous, and she was edgy over the attention they received. Still she wasn't sorry she had come. Some of the children came close and touched her hair and rubbed their rough hands over her skin. Philip's mother was receiving the same attention, and Hayley tried to follow her example and ignore them, but she shrank from their touch.

They were served food from a large pot. The stew was tasty, and Hayley was hungry, but she could hardly swallow. What awaited them? When she felt Philip's eyes upon her, she ate all she'd been given, for she didn't want to embarrass him before these people.

She was also uncomfortable when she caught Nonna looking at Philip. She might be taking Saponi, but it didn't take much discernment to know that the girl wanted Philip. *And if I hadn't come here, he'd have taken her*.

The wedding ceremony turned out to be quite simple, and Hayley couldn't imagine that the family would have been invited for such an ordinary event. Saponi and Nonna stood before the shaman of the tribe, who danced around them muttering a few incantations before he took a long string of wampum from Nonna's hand. With it, he struck her and Saponi on their right shoulders and handed the beads to Saponi. That was all.

Dancing started soon, and Hayley joined the women on one side of the circle, feeling lonely and afraid. Calling on all the will power she had inherited from her courageous ancestor who had gone unafraid to her execution, Hayley stood tall and proud.

She watched the dance with interest as the men jumped and cavorted in the circle, contorting their bodies in animal-like gestures, swaying and panting. The only music came from the gourd rattles they shook rhythmically. The men began to draw women into the dance, prancing around them while they stood.

What will I do if one chooses me? The role of the women seemed simple enough, but what would Philip want her to do? She switched worried eyes to his, and he was watching her. A slight nod of his head seemed to indicate that she should join the dancers if asked.

She wasn't surprised when Saponi approached her, beckoning, and again she glanced at Philip, whose expression had hardened, but she followed his brother among the sweating, swaying dancers. Her hands trembled, and the dust stirred up by the moving feet choked her.

She suffered through the remainder of the dance, not understanding the words that Saponi muttered to her as he danced around her, but mistrusting the expression on his face. When the dancers dropped to their knees, the women left the circle, and custom or not, Hayley moved in Philip's direction. When he saw her intentions, he moved to the left of the men's circle, so even though they stood side-by-side, she remained theoretically with the women.

Hayley reached a hand to Philip, and he grasped it firmly. Even in the worst hours during her flight from England, she had never felt so completely surrounded by enemies.

An expectant hush fell over the crowd when a man wearing a headdress of eagle feathers, and draped in a fur cape, entered the circle. Hayley couldn't see him well because dusk had settled over the village, but she felt the power of his presence and detected his significant gaze toward her and Philip.

"Opechancanough," Philip muttered quietly, when the chief's attention turned to Maggie and Towaye. Hayley moved closer to Philip, and she was reassured by the tightening of his hand on hers. If any safety existed for her in this village, Philip would provide it.

Opechancanough beckoned, and the women joined him.

"What are they doing now?" Hayley whispered.

He shook his head and didn't answer. Hayley gasped, and she felt Philip stiffen beside her, when two bound men were shoved from a nearby lodge. The men were Europeans, and Philip drew her back into the shadow.

"So this is why we were summoned here," he muttered in an undertone.

Sensing his need for silence, Hayley didn't reply. The women in the circle, holding clubs and rocks, lined up in two rows, facing each other about three feet apart. The two men were brought near the women, so that the light from a fire fell upon their faces, and Hayley gasped again. One of the men was Jacques Guise!

"Say nothing," Philip commanded in a whisper. "Don't forget Saponi can understand."

At the head of the line of women, Guise's feet were untied, and he was moved forward, hands still secured by leather thongs. When he ran between the two rows of women, blow after blow rained upon his head and shoulders. Bruised and bleeding, Guise fell in a heap not far from where Hayley stood, and Philip stepped in front of her. Then the Indians began to chant, brandishing their war clubs and muskets angrily.

"What are they saying?" she whispered.

Philip hesitated a moment, glancing around to see if they were being watched. "Death to the English invaders."

No sound escaped Hayley's lips, but she knew, if this whole village turned on them, Towaye and Philip could do little, despite their prowess. Not since the night before she left England had Hayley remembered the words of the psalmist, "I will say of the Lord, he is my refuge and my fortess: my God; in him will I trust." Those words brought her the same comfort as in England almost a year ago. If she were to die at the hands of these Indians, she'd die courageously.

"Philip, no matter what happens to us here, I want you to know that I'm not sorry you married me, and I'm thankful for the days we've spent together."

He put his arm around her, and she felt his body tremble. "That great love I talked about . . . I feel that way about you, my dearest one. I should have told you before, but something always seemed to stop my lips."

But Opechancanough apparently intended them no harm at that time, for when the two wounded men were dragged away, the crowd dispersed. Saponi directed his family to a nearby lodge and left them.

The four of them looked silently at each other, and Philip directed a question to his father in sign language. By the dim light filtering into the room from an outside fire, Hayley saw Towaye throw out his arms expressively, implying a need for silence.

Philip took a deerskin from his pack and placed it on the bare earth for Hayley. He covered her tenderly with a bear skin, then lay down between her and the door. Although quiet reigned inside the building, Hayley could hear activity throughout the village. Dogs barked and growled, footsteps plodded by their lodge, and Hayley kept her eyes glued to the uncovered doorway. She could see the legs of an Indian, who stood guard a few feet from the lodge. Occasionally, someone would peer in the door.

The scent from the bearskin was nauseating, and as her tension increased, Hayley gasped for breath. She sat up, and at the movement, Philip spoke softly, "What's the matter?"

She could see by the faint light that his eyes were alert and wakeful. "I'm afraid," she answered.

He reached to touch her arm. "I'm not going to sleep, and I doubt Father will either. You'll be all right. Try to rest."

Hayley eased back down on the bed, but kept turning under the odorous skin until Philip moved over on the mat with her and drew her into his arms. He lifted the bearskin until it covered both their bodies. Hayley snuggled close to him and sighed, "That's better."

"I'm not sure it's better for me, for I must keep alert to what's going on here. I can't do that with you in my arms."

"What is happening?" Hayley whispered. "I understood your need for silence when we were among the others, but if we whisper, no one will hear."

"When they brought out those two white men and made them run the gauntlet, I suspected why we were summoned to come here. First of all, they wanted to see if Father and I would interfere, and they may want to warn the English to leave."

"Do you think they know Jacques Guise is my kinsman?"

"I'd like to know the answer to that question. Because I prefer to think so, I'm going to believe that was just a coincidence. He just happened to be one of the settlers they captured."

"Is there any way we can help them?"

"I've been trying to think how. If Father and I were alone, we might attempt a rescue, but it's too risky with you and Mum here. If I can interpret Father's silent message, he intends to leave here as soon as possible in the morning. And that means a long trip tomorrow, so you must go to sleep." He started to move away from her.

Hayley put her arms around him. "Please don't leave me. I'll go to sleep easier if I can touch you."

Philip hesitated. "Don't you know how difficult this is for me, Hayley?" Even while they had talked, Hayley had been conscious of Philip's nearness, and that his emotions were being stirred by her presence. She knew she was just as safe if he lay four feet away as nestled in his arms, but she needed this man—his strength, his love, his devotion.

Suddenly Philip rolled away from Hayley, as two Indians, one of them Saponi, burst into the room, lighted pine torches held high in their hands. Fear quickly replaced the almost-magic moment. Towaye and Philip stood together to confront the intruders.

In English, Saponi growled, his eyes wild with unrestrained passion, "Have you been out of this building?"

"Ask the guard," Philip retorted. "He has been watching the door. I haven't left the room."

Saponi's gaze swung to his father. "Nor I, my son."

Still speaking in English, he said, "Don't leave this lodge. These people have gone wild." Hayley sensed he was truly concerned for his family. "The two settlers have escaped. Opechancanough thought one of you might have helped them."

"You have our word. None of us have slept, but we have not contacted the prisoners," Towaye answered. "We did not know they were here until they were brought to run the gauntlet."

Saponi nodded in relief, Hayley thought, and exited as quickly as he had come. If Philip's parents hadn't slept, they must have been aware of the scene between her and their son, and her cheeks grew warm.

"Now what do we do?" Philip asked Towaye.

"We do nothing tonight. Saponi is right; it would not be safe for us to venture outside. In the morning, first light, we're leaving. I won't risk my Maggie or Hayley any longer."

With the commotion going on outside the lodge, the two men must have thought they were safe to talk. "Do you think the presence of the two settlers is the reason they wanted us to come here?"

Towaye nodded sagely. "Trouble is coming between the Indians and English. Only by the grace of God will we avoid it. We must try to rest. If you'll keep watch the first part of the night, I'll take the morning watch."

Philip nodded agreement, and Towaye and Maggie lay down on the mat. Drawing Hayley into his arms, Philip kissed her eyes, her forehead, and lastly her lips.

"I'll never forgive them for breaking in here. Will you ever really belong to me?"

"I know the interruption was a good thing. Events, not only here, but in England threaten our happiness, and if Jacques Guise saw us among the Indians, now that he's escaped, he'll take the news back to Jamestown. If God wants us to be together, surely by spring we should know."

"But spring will not come for a long time," Philip said, and Hayley could hear defeat in his voice.

He sat down with his back to the wall of the lodge, facing the door, with a nod for her to lie down. Knowing he was on guard, Hayley went to sleep, but not before she thought long upon his statement. *Gentle spring, come quickly,* was her last reflection.

They were required the next morning to have an audience with Opechancanough. They entered his lodge, where he sat on a high dias with a red fox cape over his shoulders. On the floor before him lay the mangled, bleeding body of one of the white prisoners. Hayley clutched at Philip's arm, but she forced herself to look at the corpse—it was not Guise's body. Had he gotten away?

"Don't let him see your fear," Philip muttered, and Hayley straightened her shoulders and stared at Opechancanough.

Hayley feared this man more than any other she had

seen. He stood to his full height, and she noted he was as tall as Philip. His features were marked by tattooed designs, and painted emblems covered his chest. He hurled verbal assaults, their nature made clear to her by Philip's rigid grasp on her arm, and the pulsing of a muscle in his jaw.

At last it was over, and they left the Indian village behind them. Not until they had walked almost an hour did Hayley question Philip.

"What did he say?"

"He's demanding we join him to destroy the Englishmen . . . promised you and Mum would be safe if we did."

"Then if you don't help him, the two of us are in danger?"

"He didn't say as much, but the inference was there."

"What did you say? Did you stall for time?"

"No, of course not. We told him we wouldn't help him. You can't bargain with Opechancanough. Oh, Hayley, how can I ever hope to make a home here when I can't bring peace between my people?"

"Would it help you if I weren't here?"

He paused his stride for a moment and took her chin in his hands. "Do you want to return to England?"

She searched his eyes, read his love for her. "No. I don't want to leave you."

She knew that was the truth. If only the other members of her family were with her, she could happily remain with this man.

Philip took her in his arms, and although his lips were gentle, Hayley experienced the same tug of emotions he exhibited.

"After last night, I couldn't let you go, if you wanted to."

chapter

8

Spring 1621

"FOR, LO, THE WINTER IS PAST, the rain is over and gone; the flowers appear on the earth; the time of the singing of birds is come, and the voice of the turtle is heard in our land," Philip had read last night from the Song of Solomon. As if his words were a harbinger of the season, Hayley opened the door, and the sweet scent of spring entered the house. She gazed out across the greening fields to the James, reflecting on the fact that more than a year had passed since she had left England. Except for the uncertainty and concern about what had happened to her loved ones there, she was satisfied with her life.

She had become a good wife to Philip in all ways except one. Hayley's love had developed to its fullest during the winter months, and she was ready to accept Philip as her husband in every meaning of the word, but for some reason, Philip was reluctant. Did he perhaps discern her royal background and deem himself unworthy to touch her?

The winter had not been cold, and they had made a few trips to Jamestown. Paula had completed their garments in early autumn, and Hayley and Philip had worn the fashionable clothing several times to the church services. And always on Sunday, whether they were in Jamestown or not, the two of them had dressed in their finery and observed the day of worship at home.

A smile flitted across Hayley's face when she remembered the delight shown when Philip had presented the blue silk gown to his mother. Towaye was silent during the first modeling, but the pride shining from his black eyes brought a tightness to Hayley's throat.

Towaye and Maggie Lawrence had visited several times through the winter, but not a word was heard from Saponi, nor any hint of an Indian uprising. "If we have an attack, it won't come before spring," Philip had said, and his father had agreed.

Although she welcomed it, Hayley often wondered if the arrival of spring would bring peace or war. And what about word from England? Surely by now, her uncle could have written to her.

As a homemaker, Hayley knew she had achieved success. The household chores were no effort at all, and considering the narrow choice of food, she had been able to make their meals tasty and nourishing. She had even helped Philip with his work. He had taught her how to strip tobacco in the fall—taking the dried leaves from the stalk, grading them into piles according to quality, tying several leaves together into "hands", and finally storing them in wooden barrels for the journey to England. She had joined him when he took his crop to Jamestown on a small shallop, and rejoiced with him when it had brought a good price from the London Company dealer. After he paid the tax levied on the settlers, he still had enough coin to hire an indentured servant when some arrived in the colony.

One Sunday afternoon in early spring, Philip and Hayley walked into the woodlands. She wore the buckskin outfit Philip's mother had given her before their visit to the Indian village. Hayley inhaled deeply of the fragrant forest, ablaze with blooming redbud as well as the white dogwood blooms just beginning to open. Underneath their feet, pastel pink and purple flowers bloomed in profusion. Birds she had never seen in England flitted through the woods before them.

When they sat beside a small woodland stream that reflected the towering evergreens and blue sky in its tree-lined course, Hayley dipped her fingers in the cold water.

"Did you tell my mother that you knew her brother, John Lawrence?"

Hayley's fingers froze. "I know who he is; I'm not really very well acquainted with him."

"But you could tell me how to contact him, couldn't you? I know Mum longs to have news of her family, but she won't communicate with them because they probably wouldn't approve of Father. They've never made any attempt to contact her all these years, so they may not know that she's living. I'm going to write to him."

Hayley's peace of mind plummeted. Just when she had decided that the New World was the place for her, this would have to happen. How could she explain to Philip that she didn't want him to contact John Lawrence?

"He would no doubt get the letter if you sent it to Exeter, Devonshire, England."

No more was said about John Lawrence as they continued their walk, but when they rushed into the house to escape a late afternoon shower, Hayley put her hand on Philip's arm and said, "Philip, please don't mention my name if you write to John Lawrence."

Philip's expression was startled. "But you said you didn't know John Lawrence!"

"But he knows me! Please don't mention that you're married to me."

"Can't you tell me why?"

With eyes lowered, she shook her head.

He lifted her chin, and forced her eyes to meet his. "Have you committed some crime? Is that why you left England?"

She shook her head vehemently. "No, that isn't it at all. I've done nothing to be ashamed of, and I'd tell you if I could, but I took an oath to remain silent about my past. It just isn't *my* secret, for the lives of many others are involved."

"Would you rather that I didn't write to him?"

"No, you owe that much to your mother. Write to him, but avoid mentioning me."

Philip allowed her to read the letter after he'd written it. Nothing in the short missive should have disturbed her, yet she saw its departure for England with misgiving.

Straightening her back to rest it from an hour's hoeing in the garden, Hayley was surprised to see Walter Johnson approaching.

"Is Paula all right?" she cried in concern.

"She's fine!" Walter answered, and a smile lit his rugged features. "And we have a hefty baby boy."

Forcing herself to be joyful for Paula and Walter, the words brought a pang to Hayley's spirit. *A baby boy!* Joy now, but what sorrow might Paula have later? The words brought poignant memories to Hayley that she thought she had successfully stifled in her mind.

Hayley laid down the hoe. "Come in, Walter. Philip is preparing the field for the tobacco plants."

"Yes, I saw him as I passed by. I can only stay a few minutes. I came to invite you to a pig pickin' we're having next Saturday to celebrate our son's birth. Paula for sure wanted you to be there. A few of us went to Hog Island, and I caught a pig. We're going to roast it and have a big celebration. You can be there, I reckon?"

"Surely," Hayley said as they entered the house. She set out a cup and plate for Walter. "That is, if Philip thinks we can leave."

She motioned Walter to the table as she brought bread she'd baked earlier in the day and a pot of honey she had helped Philip take from a tree in midwinter. "Have something to eat, Walter, before you start back." She brewed a pot of tea.

Walter looked approvingly around the room. Because of Paula's condition, neither of the Johnsons had visited Philip and Hayley. "You've made a right nice housewife, Hayley. Paula was worried about you . . . she didn't think you'd been used to doing for yourself."

Pouring a cup of tea for Walter, and one for herself, she sat at the table with him. Smilingly she said, "She was right, of course, and I was a miserable failure until I finally learned. Philip is a patient man, and he didn't complain. But enough about me; I want to hear about the baby. What have you named him?"

"Walter, Jr.," he said, and a smile lighted his face. "And Paula thinks he's a wonderful baby. She's wantin' you to see him. Do you know anything about babies?"

Hayley hesitated. "Well, yes, I do . . ." Hearing Philip's steps at the door, she turned. "Oh, you're in early."

"I could smell that bread down by the river."

Hayley laughed, relieved that he'd interrupted the talk about babies. "Sit down. I'll bring you a plate."

After Walter and Philip had consumed a whole loaf of bread, they leaned back to discuss the affairs of the colony.

"How're you doing in your campaign to win a seat in the House of Burgesses? Ain't that supposed to be decided soon?"

"Next month. I've talked to many people, but I don't know if I'll be chosen, for there's a man over on Martin's Hundred who's trying for the seat too."

Hesitantly, Walter said, "I think I should tell you that Jacques Guise has been spreading talk about you. Says when he was a prisoner of the Pamunkeys last fall that he saw you there acting like you was right at home."

Hayley sensed the tautness of Philip's body. "I was there all right, but not willingly. If those stories are spread around this area, it won't help my election."

"Sure hope you do get elected. That would give you more reason to come to Jamestown. Paula likes to have you visit. We're buildin' on a new room . . . thought with the little one, we could use more space."

"Anything else interesting going on in the colony?"

"Oh, more loads of people comin' in every week, and settlements are spreading all along the James. You haven't had any trouble with anyone claiming your land, have you?"

"No, and I don't think we will since the Burgesses recognized Mum as one of the 'old settlers.' On a map in Jamestown we're listed as Lawrence's plantation. Being right next to Martin's Hundred, and without much unclaimed land on the other side, I think our holding is safe enough."

"Big doin's up around Henrico now. George Thorpe was in Jamestown last week, and he's all excited about the college he's buildin' for the Indians. Says he hopes to have a building ready for next year. He's real chummy with this Opechancanough. Thinks the Indians are friendly and all." With a piercing look in Philip's direction, he continued, "What do you know about Opechancanough?"

Hayley observed the lines of tension develop around Philip's mouth and across his lips, and unobserved by Walter, she placed a hand on her husband's knee. He flashed her a look of gratitude.

"Walter, I'm having a hard time trying to be an English planter but still retain some loyalty to the natives. I'm talking to you as a friend, and I'd prefer that you don't repeat what I say." Another long hesitation. "Opechanca-nough hates all whites . . . I think he's planned revenge since the confrontation he had with John Smith years ago, when Smith insulted him and humbled him before his people. Sufficient to say, the English are getting too friendly with the natives, you know, trusting them too much, allowing them to be armed."

"My sentiments exactly," Walter agreed, and he pounded his hand on the table. "The Indians wander in and out of Jamestown fort unchallenged. The London officials believe they're friendly, and that the whites have the natives outnumbered."

Remembering the crowd at Opechancanough's village last fall, Hayley doubted that.

"Guise said hundreds of armed Indians were at Opechancanough's settlement, but because Guise is a Frenchman and a Catholic, most of the English settlers ignore him. But it alarms me, Philip."

"You have reason to be alarmed," Philip agreed as Walter rose to leave.

When Walter passed out of hearing, Hayley said, "At least we know Guise escaped."

"Yes, but for our sakes, it might have been just as well if he hadn't. Somehow I distrust him as much as I do Opechancanough."

"The baby is adorable, Paula," Hayley cried as she cuddled the little one against her breast and snuggled her head against him.

Rocking back and forth in the wooden chair that Walter had made for Paula, Hayley crooned a lullaby to the baby. Her eyes contained a faraway expression, and Philip eyed her intently, marveling that she handled the baby with ease and the hand of experience.

Hayley lifted her eyes and felt Philip's gaze upon her, his

eyes full of questions. Had her handling of Paula's son given him a clue to her past? Philip should have a son. If she could only be the wife he needed!

Later in the day, alone in the house with the baby while Paula went to the garden, Hayley was surprised at a furtive knock at the door. When she answered, she stared in surprise at Jacques Guise, who brushed past her and into the house without an invitation.

"You are alone?" he queried in his accented English.

"But just for a moment. What do you want?"

He thrust a letter toward her. "For you. Many weeks ago, it arrived, in a letter for me. An answer your uncle desires. In two days a ship leaves for London. The answer must be on it."

"But how can I get the letter to you? My husband knows nothing about the situation in England."

"I vil vatch. When you go out, have the letter in your hand; I vil be nearby to take it."

"But what about paper?" Hayley cried in agitation. "I haven't seen any writing materials in the colony."

"The answer is urgent." He opened the door and slipped away as secretively as he had come. Looking down the street toward the fort, Hayley saw Philip heading toward the Johnsons' house. She only hoped he hadn't seen Guise. Noticing that Paula was still in the garden, Hayley broke the seal on the envelope.

> Soon after you left we learned that John Lawrence was not the one who betrayed us to the king's men, but rather one of our own men, Arnold Wright. As of now, your father and Roger are still in the Tower.

119

And Arnold Wright had watched her departure from England! The letter had been written in September of last year; much could have happened in that time. She peered out the window and saw that Philip had stopped to talk to a man on the street. She quickly scanned the rest of the letter.

> Our followers are still eager to claim the throne, so I urge you to return to England as soon as you can book passage. Choose a reliable boat and captain. Once we are in control, we can release the prisoners from the Tower. The fate of your family may depend on your quick action.

Hearing Philip's voice as he spoke to Paula, Hayley stuck the note in the pocket of her apron. She loved her new husband, but she could not further abandon her son. Already she had failed little Roger by leaving him imprisoned in the Tower with her father. He must think she had no love or concern for him. What was she to do?

Long after the rest of the household had settled for the night, Hayley lay awake in the bed she shared with Paula and the baby. With her hand patting the form of the infant beside her, Hayley's mind turned to the birth of her own son seven years ago—the one bright memory in her political marriage to Robert Grover. When Robert had been killed the night before she'd left London, Hayley hadn't felt any grief, only fear for her son's safety. A sleepless night brought no answer to her dilemma.

As she dressed the next morning, Hayley smoothed the green silk dress over her layer of petticoats. When had any of the elaborate gowns she'd worn in England given her the pleasure of this garment? Daringly, Hayley pulled the gold cross, once the possession of Mary, Queen of Scots, from inside her bodice and arranged it on the lace collar.

When Philip entered the room, he looked inquiringly at her display of the cross. She had often worn it openly when they were alone at the plantation, but as far as he knew, no one else in the colony had seen the precious possession. He nodded approval.

Philip's garments pleased her, too, for he had emerged from the loft dressed in leather breeches and a doublet made from brown broadcloth. His buckled shoes were the new ones that he'd made the previous winter.

"Oh, husband," Hayley exclaimed. "You're so handsome." He caught her close.

"Am I really your husband, Hayley?"

Her pulse raced, but Paula bustled into the room, and she didn't reply.

Hurrying around to help Paula, Hayley placed dishes of food on the tables. Dried vegetables had been used because the gardens didn't yet have any fresh produce, except for a few green onions, and Hayley sniffed their pungent odor as she carried the food. For dessert Paula had prepared a large tub of syllabub, a colonial treat made of cider and milk, flavored with sugar and fresh strawberries.

The pig was roasting on a spit which the men turned over a bed of glowing embers. When the meat was browned a rich golden color, and juices were seeping into the bed of coals, Walter decided that the meat was ready. Several of the men helped him lift the carcass to a large wooden slab, and he invited his guests to help themselves to the food. Because of the scarcity of eating utensils, each family had brought its own, and the people piled their plates full of Paula's vegetables and pulled off tempting morsels of meat with their fingers.

Hayley found it hard to eat, her mind whirling with the knowledge gleaned from the letter from England. In a sudden fit of loneliness, she looked around for Philip and saw him sitting with a middle-aged man under an oak tree, which was providing welcome shade in the Johnsons' yard. He motioned for her to join them. Philip and the man rose when she came near.

"Mr. Thorpe, this is my wife, Hayley," Philip said. "Hayley, Mr. Thorpe is in charge of the college lands, where facilities will be built to educate Indian children."

Thorpe, a slender man, smiled at Hayley from a wrinkled face topped by a thatch of white hair.

"Oh, I can see into the future," he said, "and envision the day when the natives and the Europeans will live together without fear of each other. Our college will be the answer to that. I'm visiting the different Indian villages encouraging them to send their young men to be educated. Since I've learned that your father is an Algonquian, I have wanted to talk with you, Mr. Lawrence. What do you think of our plan?"

"Your intentions are to turn the Indians to the English culture, I suppose?"

"Yes, yes, of course. The Indians must be taught our way of life, our religion, our type of government, our superior culture."

"I think I should warn you that the Indians will not willingly give up their way of life. If not for my mother's influence, I'm sure I would not be interested in English ways."

"But I have talked with Opechancanough, who seems to be a leader of the tribes, and he's pledged to maintain peace between the Indians and the English. We have a friendly relationship. Some of our workers are now building a home for him, for he is impressed by our structures. You see, he *wants* to take on our ways."

"Especially interested in procuring swords, muskets, and gunpowder?" Philip asked pointedly. "The rule of this colony was once that the natives would not be given firearms. Now they have as many muskets as the English."

"But only for hunting, my boy. Or for defense. No, I'm convinced that we'll have full cooperation from the natives." He gave Hayley an admiring look. "Just to see the happiness of your dear wife proves to me that this colony will only be the better for joining our two races. And, by the way, what part of England do you come from, my dear?"

"I was born in London." That was enough for him to know, she thought.

"Then you'll be interested to know that sometime next month, a string ensemble from London with a lute, cello, and violin will be coming to perform in the colony. I hope to use their visit as a way to raise support for the college. If no one has any coin to pledge, perhaps they can promise some of their next tobacco crop or a few days' labor."

"That sounds wonderful! I've missed the music of England. I once played the lute, but that was far away in another life. I've probably forgotten the skill of it now, but I'd enjoy hearing someone else play."

Their attention was diverted by Walter, who called his guests around him. "Everybody remember how to play charades? Let's try to recall some of the fun of merry old England through some."

The afternoon's fun was lively, and everyone seemed to welcome a break from the rugged routine of daily existence. But the last charade enacted the beheading of Mary, Queen of Scots. The mockery of the crowd brought a pallor to Hayley's face when Paula, who represented the ill-fated queen, walked slowly to the place of execution. And when Paula laid her head on the block, and the make-believe ax fell, Hayley uttered a pitiful shriek and fainted. Philip caught her in his arms before she toppled to the ground, and as he took her into the house, his eyes intercepted the mocking gaze of Jacques Guise.

Philip had no sooner laid Hayley on the bed than she opened her eyes. "What is it, dearest?" he whispered.

Slowly the horror of the scene penetrated Hayley's consciousness, and she reached her arms to him. "Hold me, Philip. I don't want to leave you. I don't want to return to England."

His arms tightened protectively, and he held her with a look that a man has for only one woman. Hayley knew that he wanted her, that he loved her, but why did he hesitate to claim her physically? Only when she was his wife in act, as well as in name, would she have the assurance that she could stay with him forever.

The incident, as terrible as it had been, was enough to give Hayley direction for the course she must follow. After Paula and the baby were sleeping, Hayley slipped from the bed and wrote a note to her uncle on a scrap of paper she'd borrowed from her friend.

Uncle Simon,
   My duty to England, and the wishes of the Douglas family, are
no longer of importance to me. I can see no future except death
or imprisonment in what you plan to do. I beg you to make every
effort to obtain Roger's release and send him to America. With
his father dead, he should be with me.

Hayley folded the letter with no confidence that her son
would be sent to her. Knowing that Roger was now heir to
the Grover lands, she doubted that her father and Simon
would give up the boy so easily, but she intended to have
her child, if she had to return to England to get him.

"I ain't seen sich a particular 'un in all my days of
bringing over these servants." The ship's captain rolled the
stump of his pipe from one side toward the other as he
rocked along on his short, stubby legs. He waved his hand
to a man standing on the other side of the boat. "Darned
particular he be, about signing an indenture. But you may
as well talk to him. He's the only 'un left as I didn't have so
many this trip. I'm leaving this port shortly, and if he ain't
signed on with some'un who'll pay his fare, I'm going to
toss the chappie into the drink when we start home."
   Philip walked toward the lanky man, the captain tagging
at his heels.
   "Towner," the captain said. "Here's Mr. Lawrence to
talk to you . . . mebbe you ain't too good to work fer him."
   The angular man swung to face Philip. He looked to be
strong enough, though he was thin. Of course, many a
man was gaunt when he arrived after a long journey from
England.
   Philip scrutinized the man closely. No scars on his hands
to indicate he'd been a prisoner. Hayley's safety was at
stake and he couldn't take a chance on a criminal.

He was under as much scrutiny as he was giving Towner, Philip realized, and for some reason, he distrusted the look from the man's bearded face. *What emotion is registered in that face? Malice? Mockery?* Long hair covered his forehead, and a bushy beard and mustache left little of his face open for inspection, and Philip decided he was overly suspicious of the man.

The captain handed Philip a sheaf of papers drawn by the London Company. "Benjamin Towner, 50 years old. Experience: laboring man and farmer, good with horses. Some carpentry." Those were the only things that interested Philip, but he did glance quickly through the rest of the contract. Towner would work for him for five years, for room and board, and at the end of that time, Philip would be obligated to provide Towner with a new outfit of clothing, three barrels of corn, and some farming tools to enable the man to provide for himself.

Philip would have preferred a servant with a wife, for he wanted Hayley to have help, but since Towner was the only one available, he decided to take him. With a servant to work in the fields, perhaps he could be free to help Hayley.

"I have a plantation east of Jamestown. If you sign an indenture with me, you will be working in tobacco fields. We have much work to do, for I want to clear more forest land for farming."

"Are you a family man, or be you single?"

"I have a wife," Philip answered shortly. "Are you interested in working for me?"

"Sounds all right to me, mate," Towner said in a servile tone that Philip thought was forced. This man didn't strike him as anybody's servant, and he hesitated. He wanted a man who had enough strength and intelligence to be a help to him, yet not one with such an independent spirit that he would run away as soon as Philip paid his fare to the New World. And there was something else. Was it distrust? But how could he possibly distrust a man he hadn't seen before?

Even after Towner placed his mark on the indenture papers, and Philip took the pen the captain handed him, his hand seemed to halt on its own. Perhaps he should have talked this over with Hayley, but shrugging off his hesitation as foolishness, he signed the indenture.

"Bring your things to the fort," he said as he handed over the necessary coin to pay Towner's passage.

Paula and Hayley were waiting beside the fort when he and Towner approached, and Hayley stared keenly at the stranger. She had a suspicion that she might have known him at one time, or at least someone who looked like him.

She was aggravated that she formed an instant dislike of the man, but she considered his gaze upon her to be bold. So much of his countenance was hidden by the heavy beard that his face, except for the eyes, was expressionless, thus she could hardly reach a fair judgment of the man so soon. Turning away from Towner and kissing Paula and the baby good-by, she started toward the plantation. *Be glad that Philip has someone to help him,* she chided herself.

chapter
9

"Two trips to Jamestown within a month. We're becoming well-traveled colonists, Philip," Hayley commented as they neared the village.

Philip had hesitated about leaving the plantation because a rainy week had delayed his work, but with Towner there now, he had decided to forget about the tobacco fields for a while. Since their last visit to Jamestown, Hayley had been quiet, somber. He could trace her despondency to the party they'd attended at Paula's. *But what had happened during the charades to upset her?* Try as he could, he hadn't been able to come up with an answer. Towner's presence might have been disturbing, but she had often insisted that he needed someone to help him.

He hoped that the trip to Jamestown would cheer her, for seeing her moping around silently doing her work had unnerved him.

He reached for her hand and answered, "Yes, we've become regular visitors at Jamestown once we started. I hope we aren't wearing out our welcome at the Johnsons'."

No reason to fear that, Hayley was sure, for Paula greeted them warmly as she always did. Her rosy cheeks were even brighter than usual as she talked excitedly. "I was hoping you'd come in for the show. Big doin's in Jamestown. No culture at all before, but tonight we're to have a concert, and the musicians have a cello, violin, and a lute. The performance will be in the church, and even that may not be big enough to hold everybody."

Philip and Hayley were immediately asked if they thought the baby had grown since their last visit. Hayley laughed at Philip's awkwardness when Paula handed Walter Jr. to him.

"He weighs about as much as a stalk of tobacco, if that's any help."

"Oh, give him to me. I'll guess his weight," Hayley said with a laugh, a sound that encouraged Philip. "He has grown, Paula, no doubt of that."

The church was already crowded when Walter found places for them on one of the front benches. Philip looked with interest at the musicians who were dressed in elaborate black broadcloth doublets with lace ruffs around the necks. Their embroidered hose, reaching from their breeches to leather boots, seemed effeminate to Philip. He admired the three stringed instruments for their finely grained wood and delicate finish, but they made whanging noises that were strange to Philip's ears. Perhaps he might grow used to the sounds, but tonight, they seemed discordant to him. Judging from the rapt look on Hayley's face, he knew she was enjoying it. His glance swept the rest of the audience, and he was surprised to see tears in the eyes of many people. They were thinking of the country they'd left behind, he surmised.

During a pause in the concert, Hayley asked the lutenist, "May I hold it a minute? It is such a beautiful instrument."

Hayley ran her hands lovingly over the smooth wood. "You're welcome to try it, ma'am," the man invited. Willingly, Hayley sat down and rested the pear-shaped instrument in her lap, while with her right hand she plucked the lower strings, and stopped the strings along the fretted neck with her left-hand fingers.

With eyes closed, and savoring the weight of the lute in her lap, Hayley recalled visits of traveling musicians to their home in London, and how she had learned to play the lute in the lonely days after she left her father's home to live as a bride in Devon and during those final days when she waited for Roger to be born. The past deluged her mind, and she thought of the letter to Simon, stating her intentions to break all ties with England.

Her reverie was interrupted by George Thorpe, the director of the college, who stood at her side, his lined face wearing a benevolent smile. "Sing for us, Mistress Lawrence. The beauty of a lady's voice will add much to our concert."

Hayley had never performed in public, and in England, it might not have been appropriate, but what could it matter here in Jamestown? In soft lilting tones, Hayley sang a selection she had learned as a child.

> Flee away with me, my love of yore,
> To the crystal fountains where we may sing
> Of days of old, when we were young
> Those moments sublime that come no more.

Opening her eyes to the applause, Hayley met Philip's compassionate gaze as she handed the lute back to the musician.

When Walter led the women from the building, Philip stayed behind. "Your music was beautiful," Paula said, "and I'm sure you encouraged people to give such a wonderful pledge to the college. It was generous of Philip to pledge three days of labor for himself."

Puzzled, Hayley answered, "But I thought he intended to pledge a hogshead of tobacco he had stored here in Jamestown with the London Company officials." *How will I ever manage to do without him for three days?*

Almost an hour lapsed before Philip arrived, and Hayley had rocked baby Walter until he slept soundly. Philip's hands were behind his back when he entered the building, but reaching out his hands to Hayley, she saw he held the lute.

"Philip!"

"I want you to have it, my dear. The troupe is returning home, and the man can buy another instrument. You have little enough pleasure, and I won't have you deprived of the music you love."

So he'd used the tobacco to buy the lute and pledged three days of his time instead—time that he couldn't afford to lose on the plantation.

Hayley put her arms around his waist. "Always sacrificing for me. You know how much you need tools and equipment on the plantation."

"But hearing you play the instrument will bring me pleasure, too."

"I do appreciate the gift, Philip, and I . . . appreciate you, too." She pulled his head down and kissed him on the cheek, but Philip dropped his lips to hers, until rosy-faced at Walter's cheering, Hayley pulled away.

Hayley feared that the days of housework might have stiffened her fingers until she could no longer play the lute, but after a few days of practice, she regained the skill she had known before. Thus another event was added to their evening ritual. After the Bible reading, Hayley played and sang for Philip before he unwound her long auburn hair and treated it to a nightly brushing.

While Philip was at Henrico working out his pledge to the college project, Hayley became aware that Benjamin Towner was a threat to her. Philip had built a small house for the man down near the barn; thus Hayley had little communication with him. Although the man hadn't revealed much of his past to Philip, he had done his work well, giving his master no cause to regret hiring the man.

Like the other planters, Philip welcomed a cheap supply of labor, since his obligations to Towner would be very little once the five years of labor was completed.

Philip had allowed Hayley to make the decision of what she would do in his absence. "I had thought, Hayley, that I would take Towner with me to the college, but I don't like to leave you here alone. I'd take you with me, but the route will be a rough one. You can stay with my parents if you'd prefer. Or you might want to go into Jamestown, if you don't want to be here with Towner nearby."

After considering all the possibilities, Hayley finally decided to stay at home. She would have enjoyed a visit with Mistress Lawrence, but the thought of encountering Saponi disturbed her. She hadn't been able to forget his visit with them last winter. He had stopped one day seeking shelter during a snowstorm. He didn't speak to her in Philip's presence, but his eyes had followed her every move.

As the two brothers visited, Saponi spoke only in Algonquian, but Philip answered him in English, and she knew it was to keep her aware of their conversation. And that night instead of going to his usual bed in the loft, he had indicated that Saponi would sleep upstairs, and Philip had rolled into a skin not far from Hayley's bed.

Saponi had lingered the next morning until Philip went to do the outside chores, and before he left, he cupped his hand under Hayley's chin. She shrank from his touch, but he held her eyes in a bold stare.

"If you were my woman, you wouldn't have to sleep alone," he said in English. "Think about it. The Indians are going to drive the white settlers into the ocean. In my lodge, you will be safe."

Hayley hadn't felt at ease again when Philip was out of her sight, and she wanted to beg him to not go to the college. She was being foolish she decided, for no doubt Towner could be relied upon to help her if trouble came.

But Philip hadn't been gone more than a few hours when Towner appeared at the door. "The master told me to look out for you. Be you needing anything?"

"No, thank you. You take care of the farm work; I'll be fine up here." He backed away reluctantly, and she closed the door. While watching his retreat through the narrow window, she decided that in spite of the heat, she didn't dare leave the door unlatched. She thought miserably as she closed the door and pulled in the latchstring, *And Philip won't be back for four days*.

Towner returned two more times that day, each time

more insistent that he should enter the house. The last time he came, she refused to open the door.

Next morning, Hayley hurried through the outside chores. The garden needed some attention, but she was afraid to stay out, and she only tended to the goats and the chickens before rushing back inside.

The second night Philip was gone, long after she had gone to bed, she heard steps stalking the house, and a hand pushed on the door. *Was it Saponi or Towner?* She crept out of bed and put on her clothes. Sitting tensely by the table, facing the door, she waited to see if the intruder would return, but she didn't hear any other sound.

Her sleepless night left her lethargic, but she tried to think of some kind of weapon. Philip had taken his musket, but she didn't know how to fire it anyway. Only the knife she used at the fireplace was a possibility. She honed the blade on a pottery bowl that Walter had given her until it was sharp and deadly, wondering if she would have the nerve to use it against an assailant.

Contemplating how she might best use the knife, she heard a knock at the door. She concealed the weapon in the folds of her skirt, and asked, in what she thought was a calm voice, "Who is it?"

"Jacques Guise."

All these months Guise had never come to the house, not until now, now that Philip was gone. Was he a threat to her also? But Guise was her cousin, and supposedly her friend.

She laid the knife on the table and opened the door.

"Is it that you are alone?" he asked upon entering.

"Yes. Why have you come?"

He drew an envelope from his pocket. "A message from England."

Hayley took the letter, noting that the sealing wax was broken. Had he read the message? She tucked the letter inside the folds of her dress, hoping to get rid of him before she read the letter.

"A long way I walk to bring your message. A cup of tea could you spare?"

She motioned him to a seat at the table and prepared the brew at the hearth. She cut a slice of bread and laid it on the plate, never turning her back on him. Why did she distrust this man? What had her uncle meant by sending her to him for protection?

"Good you cook, for a queen." When Hayley frowned, he laughed. "Your dear husband, does he not know your identity? What do you think he will do when he finds out who he married? Perhaps send you to England to collect the reward?"

Hayley caught the edge of the table for support. "What do you mean by that?"

Gesturing toward her pocket with the piece of bread he held, he said, "Read the letter. You vil see."

"So you have read my personal correspondence!"

He shrugged his shoulders, and since he apparently had no notion of leaving soon, Hayley drew the thin sheet of paper from her pocket.

Hayley,

Although I will never understand what possessed you to marry a total stranger, under the circumstances, you may have made the wisest move. Your father has been executed in the Tower of London, but we were able to secure Roger's release, with the promise that the boy be taken from England.

If you haven't already told your husband of your past, you are released from the vow I took from you before you left England. I have heard some people may be searching for you in America to return you here, so take care. With the different name you now have, you may be able to find safety in America. Within a fortnight I will leave England to bring Roger to you. The future of the Douglas family may well be in America since we have none here anymore. Do not entertain any idea of returning to England. Trust God for your safety.

Simon

Hayley's joy to know that her son was safe and would be reunited with her was dimmed by the news of her father's death. She turned her back on Guise, not wanting to share her grief with anyone. And now she was faced with the task of explaining her complicated family background to Philip. How could she assure him that she truly loved him? She didn't want him to think she was staying with him only to escape persecution in England.

Hayley knew this was not the time to succumb to grief or musings, so she turned and looked directly at Guise. "Do you know of anyone who is searching for me?"

He shrugged his shoulders again, spreading his hands wide in a gesture typical of his countrymen. "How would I know? But for a price, many might return you to England. As I hear it, King James had no love for his sainted mother, so he would be glad to imprison anyone who looks like her."

"How do you know I look like her?" Hayley retorted.

"A few times, I saw the lady. She spent much time in France. And the king would not like any threat to his throne."

Hayley raised her hand for silence, for she had detected a shadow passing the window.

A knock sounded at the door. "Who is it?" Hayley asked. "Benjamin Towner."

Hayley opened the door a crack. Towner did his best to peer around her to see who was in the room.

"Need any help, milady?" he asked in his usual, servile, irritating tone. Again she had the faint stirring of memory. Somewhere in the past she had known this man. The term "milady" seemed familiar. Towner looked at her boldly, as if daring her to recognize him.

"Of course not," she replied sharply. "I told you before I'd let you know if I needed any help." He backed away, and she shut the door. Half expecting him to peer in the window, she waited until she heard his receding steps before she returned to the table where Guise sat. She made no explanation, not really knowing which one she distrusted most, Towner or Guise.

"The sainted grandmother," Guise said, as if they had not been interrupted, "how she would feel to know you had deserted the true faith to marry a Protestant heathen?"

"Religious quarrels! Why must Christians argue? Long before I came to America, I'd grown weary of such bickering, and now that I've seen the faith in God Philip and his family experience, I'm even more aware that God is not pleased with quarreling Christians. 'God is no respecter of persons: but in every nation he that feareth him, and worketh righteousness, is accepted with him.'"

"But how is it that a member of the Scottish Royal House could cohabit with a savage?"

Hayley's hazel eyes glinted angrily, and she fingered the knife on the table. "Don't speak so of my husband."

138

The next two days dragged for Hayley. She read Simon's letter over and over, and when she wasn't pondering its contents, she was peering out the window and wondering what Towner was doing, wondering if already the king's men were looking for her, wondering when Philip would return.

Four nights after he had gone, Hayley was awakened by a gentle tapping on the door. A hand flew to her throat, her voice paralyzed. Clutching the covers around her, she sat up.

"Hayley, are you awake?"

With a glad cry, she jumped from bed, and her bare feet pattered across the floor. Undoing the latch, she caught his hand and pulled him inside. Throwing her arms around him, she sobbed, "Oh, Philip, I'm glad you're home."

"Why, my dearest, what's wrong? Have you had trouble?"

Nothing was wrong now that he had returned. "Oh, it's just that I missed you. Philip, don't leave me again."

He patted her lovingly on the shoulder, acutely conscious of her curves through the folds of her thin chemise. Her body molded to his in a provocative way, and with difficulty, Philip moved away from her. He unslung the musket from his shoulder and placed it over the fireplace.

Hayley stirred up the fire. "Hungry?"

"A little." His greatest hunger was for her, and he feasted his eyes upon the picture she made in the white garment, long hair hanging over her shoulders as she placed some cold bread and cheese upon the table.

His hunger for food sated, Philip reluctantly climbed to his bed in the loft. Hayley reluctantly let him go. The hour was too late to divest her soul of its past, but by tomorrow night, she and Philip would have no secrets between them.

All the next day Hayley pondered upon the best way to tell Philip. Moving around the house preparing his favorite food, she thought of many ways to acquaint him with her past, and the destiny she had once envisioned. After the work was done for the day, Hayley dressed in her second-best outfit that Paula had made for her. She wanted the occasion to be one both she and Philip would remember. Surely tonight he would truly make her his wife.

At least he would if he wasn't angry about all the secrets she had kept from him. How could she best broach the subject?

Philip complimented the meal and her appearance, but seemed unusually quiet for a man who had been away for several days. He read the Bible aloud to her as she washed the utensils and prepared the fireplace for the next morning. After she finished her work, Hayley went to sit opposite him at the table. He closed the Bible, laid it aside, took her hand, and looked gravely at her.

"Hayley, I'm not going to insult you by being suspicious, but Towner said Jacques Guise came here while I was gone. Or at least, from his description, I assume it was Guise."

Hayley flushed angrily. "Well, I would have preferred to have told you myself, which I was planning to do tonight. You won't believe that now. I didn't tell you last night, because we have much to discuss, and I knew you needed to rest."

"Of course, I believe what you tell me."

Still angry, Hayley continued, "I'm not pleased that Guise seemed to be spying on the place and came here after you left, but I'm angrier with Towner. He kept coming here around the house, pestering me. I'm afraid of him, Philip."

"Probably I shouldn't have trusted a man we know so little about, but I couldn't think of any other way. I thought he was preferable to no protection at all."

"Let's forget him for the time being." A minute became two as Hayley searched for words. The only sound in the room was the gentle snapping of the dying coals in the fireplace. "I love you, Philip. You're the only man I have ever loved."

Philip's eyes lighted in a way Hayley had never seen before, and the table presented too large a barrier for him. With one swift movement, he came to her side and drew her upward into his arms. The moment was not made for words, and his lips held hers until she pulled away, breathless from the emotion he stirred within her.

When her lips were free, she leaned back, still secure in the circle of his arms. "But," she continued, wanting to lower her eyes from his contented gaze, but wanting more to note his expression when she said, "I have been married before."

He smiled slightly. "I know."

"You know!" she cried. "All these months, I've dreaded telling you. How did you know?"

Carrying her to the large chair, he settled her on his lap. "Let's say, I suspected. But before I tell you why I thought so, I want to know. Do you still have a husband living in England?"

"Still living! Oh, no, Philip. He was killed the day before I left England to come to Virginia."

Philip's eyes mirrored relief, and he kissed her again. "That's the reason I haven't insisted that you 'share my blanket.' I feared that you might have another husband living, and I didn't want you to have to cope with that problem."

"But what made you think that?"

He rubbed the back of her neck as he talked, and she moved her head gently to the soothing pressure of his hand. "Several things. First of all, you're twenty-five years old . . . long past the age when most women marry. And you're beautiful . . . not likely you would have escaped being married. I've thought much about your shock when you learned you had married me. I remembered how readily you took your vows, as if you'd said them before. Then in those days of unconsciousness when you first came, you would often call 'Roger,' and I assumed that was a husband. And I was sure beyond any doubt when I saw you hold Paula's baby the first time. Pain and sorrow crossed your face, and the way you lovingly cuddled the boy, I knew that you had borne a child."

"And you don't mind?"

"I would have preferred, of course, that you hadn't known any other man except me, but I can't change the past. I accepted you as you were; for you see, my dearest, for many months I've held for you that great love that I've always wanted to find with some woman. I love you, too."

When her lips were free again, Hayley leaned against Philip and sighed deeply. "How often I've wanted to share the past with you, Philip, but I was under vow to reveal nothing to anyone in the New World. My past has been full of mystery and problems, but Jacques Guise brought me a letter this week releasing me from that vow. Do you have time to listen to a long story?"

"You've already told me what I wanted most to hear. You love me, and you don't belong to any other man. I need to know only one more thing. Are you willing to stay here in Virginia and truly become my wife?"

The acceptance in her eyes might have been answer enough, but she said, "I want to stay here and become your wife in every sense of the word."

Philip raised to a slight sitting position and laughed softly at Hayley beside him. Her eyes were closed, and a slight smile infused her features. He pinched her side. "I thought you had a story to tell me. I can listen just as well in bed as anywhere."

With an effort, Hayley came back to the present. "I was married when I was fifteen . . . a political union, arranged by my father. I had no voice in the matter; it was a duty to perform for my country, and I accepted without question. He was Lord Robert Grover, a man much older than I. Our liaisons were not . . . frequent, and nothing that transpired prepared me for the ecstasy I've reached with you. Marriage is more than a meeting of flesh . . . it has to be mind and spirit, too.

"And Roger is not my husband, but my seven-year-old son." Throughout the rest of the night, Hayley explained her heritage, her relationship to the Scots queen, her slight claim to the throne of England, the failure of the plot, Robert's death, and her forced exile from England. At last she told him about the letter from Simon, and that he was bringing Roger to her.

"Will you mind taking him in, Philip? I want to have sons for you, but Roger is mine ... I love him, too."

"Do you think I would do otherwise? When the boy comes, he will be *our* son. And as for those who would try to take you back to England, never fear, I'm fighting for you now."

chapter

10

WHEN HIS TOBACCO PLANTS WERE SET OUT and the corn planted, Philip began visiting most of the residents of Martin's Hundred to enlist their support for his appointment to the House of Burgesses. Maggie Lawrence's land, adjacent to Martin's Hundred, would entitle Philip to represent that region in Jamestown.

On election day, Philip asked Hayley to accompany him to Wolstenholme Towne, the central village of Martin's Hundred, where the settlers had cleared trees along the James to build their town. Although Philip had visited the village before, Hayley had not, and she looked with interest at the fort that had been built to serve the whole community as a refuge from attack. In the company compound, a long house had been built for the unmarried men, and a storehouse adjoined it. Scattered along the dusty streets were several houses, and in the center of town was the newly built church, where the voting was to take place.

Hayley left Philip to visit with several women who were sitting on benches inside the palisade. But though she enjoyed the conversation, Hayley couldn't get her mind off the voting. Her greatest wish at the moment was that Philip would be selected as a Burgess because it was such an important matter to him.

One look at his face when he joined her for the long walk home told her he had not been chosen. He walked erect, proudly, and smiled as he greeted the other women, but she knew; the hurt was in his eyes.

They walked silently out of Wolstenholme Towne. At first Hayley's throat was too tight for words, but when they entered the forest, she reached for his hand. "I'm sorry, Philip."

He drew her into a tight embrace, and his words were muffled in her hair. "I thought I was finally overcoming the prejudice, but it surfaced again. The voting was close, but I overheard someone comment, 'He might be all right, but you can't forget that he's the same blood as these other savages, and I hear tell he's been seen in Opechancanough's village. No tellin' what he might do.'"

"Philip, you're important to me. Doesn't matter whether you're a Burgess or not. I love you."

He held her hand as they continued their journey. "But I want to establish some background so that our children won't have to fight the way I have to become recognized as a *person*. I want our descendants to be proud of their Algonquian heritage as well as their English blood. I want them to realize that there was nothing inferior about me."

"Be assured that we *will* be leaving them quite a heritage, Philip. My royal grandmother and your grandmother as leader of her clan will make our children proud of us."

Hayley was cutting corn off the cob to dry for winter use, but she was also trying to think of some way to help Philip. He had been despondent since their return from Wolstenholme Towne.

"We'll have a party," she said aloud as the thought emerged. Surely she was competent to plan some type of social event, but on second thought, *What if no one comes? That would be a worse blow to Philip.*

During her next visit in Jamestown, Hayley asked Paula, "If we have a party, do you think anyone would come? I don't want Philip to be embarrassed."

"You plan the party, and I'll see that some people attend. We have several friends who will come if I ask them."

Hayley enlisted Maggie Lawrence's help in preparing for the party and could sense Maggie's excitement over the chance to wear the blue silk gown Paula had made for her. Up until now she had worn the dress only in her home for Towaye's delight.

Although Towaye had declined to attend the party, he did go into the forest with Philip to bring in a deer and several grouse for the women to cook. Towaye and Mistress Lawrence came two days early, the first time they had stayed overnight with Philip and Hayley.

"Oh, I do hope we have enough food," Hayley repeated again. The table was loaded with pots of vegetables, stews, and puddings. Dried fruit tarts were arranged on the mantle, ready for serving.

Towaye had carved extra bowls, and he entered the house with three more of them. "If you think this will be enough, Daughter, then I will go."

"Please stay with us," Hayley begged. "It will mean much to Philip to have you here."

He nodded his head. "Yes, he has told me; perhaps I stay for a time. If I do not like, I will go into the forest."

Hayley squeezed his hand. "That's fair enough."

"I do not want the three of you to be ashamed of me," he said, voicing a concern that Hayley had already suspected.

"Never!" his wife assured him with a kiss. "As far as I'm concerned, you'll be the handsomest man here, Philip included."

The guests had been invited for the noon meal, and as the time drew nearer, Hayley's hands twitched nervously. For herself she didn't care; she'd had all the adulation she needed for a lifetime, but for Philip's sake, the guests must come.

With a leap of her spirit, she looked out across the field where a shallop loaded with people was pulling into their small landing. Fifteen men and women stepped from it, and behind, Hayley could see another boat heaving into view.

"They came! They came!" she shouted joyously. Smoothing down the white apron over her green silk gown, she took one last look in the mirror. Her hair was in place, and the emerald and ruby cross was displayed above the boned, laced bodice.

Philip appeared at the door dressed in a gray velvet doublet and breeches. His eyes were gleaming proudly as he raised his arm to Hayley. She placed her hand on it, and they moved out to meet their guests.

If Philip was diffident about greeting the people from Jamestown, he didn't show it, for Hayley, remembering the times she'd attended social gatherings in England, had coached him on the way a host and hostess should conduct themselves. Apparently at ease himself, he soon had his guests chatting freely. Before the day was over, Hayley felt most of the guests had forgotten that Philip's father was an Indian, despite the fact that Towaye spent the full day with them. Walter Johnson, in particular, made an effort to converse with Towaye, not simply out of politeness, Hayley was sure, but because he truly wanted to make Towaye's acquaintance.

After the sumptuous meal was consumed, Walter produced a game he had brought with him. He had made the simple device—a wooden ball attached by a string to a stick surmounted by a shallow pottery cup. The women watched the men's obvious enjoyment as the stick was held, cup uppermost, in their left hands, while with the right, they attempted to move the stick so that the ball would swing and be caught in the cup. Even Towaye was persuaded to try his skill at the game, and although it was the first time he had tried such a feat, he was successful time and again in seating the ball in the cup. Noting the delighted smile on his wife's face, Hayley lowered her eyelid in a slight wink to Philip.

"Do you remember any dance steps you used to enjoy in England?" Hayley asked Maggie as she brought out the lute.

For several hours she played while the guests experimented with unpracticed English dances. It might have looked comical to an English visitor to see the settlers leaping and prancing in their finery on the barren ground beside the crude house, but it was serious business to those who, for the moment, were able to put aside the rigors of New World living to enjoy a bit of nostalgia. As Hayley watched them dance, her eyes misted, remembering all the good things they'd left behind, but she knew most of them felt as she did—the goal they sought was worth the sacrifice of the moment.

With a glance at Philip, who was learning a new dance under Paula's guidance, Hayley's pulse quickened. She loved him, and as his wife, she would contribute to the future of Virginia. Towaye absolutely refused to participate in the dancing, but Mistress Lawrence, resplendent in the blue silk gown, her golden hair gleaming in the bright sun, enjoyed learning the gilliard, a quick dance of five steps with alternating movements of prancing and trotting. Although she was breathless at the end of the dance, Hayley observed the happiness on her face as she sought a place beside Towaye, whose arm was waiting to draw her close.

Two hours before sunset the guests departed so they could be safely home before nightfall. When Hayley and Philip saw the last shallop pass from sight, Philip pulled her into his arms.

"I love you," he said fervently, and Hayley needed no other thanks for the day's work.

"We will make this an annual event at Haywood, Philip. Our children will also celebrate this day, but never again will it bring the happiness afforded today."

Philip was the first to see the well-dressed Englishman, accompanied by Walter Johnson, arriving on the trail from Jamestown. Towner was working by his side as they cut the first of the tobacco stalks.

"That must be Hayley's uncle," he said aloud. "But where is the boy?"

He hardly noticed that Towner quickly ducked into the nearby tobacco barn.

"Company for you, Philip," Walter called as he raised his hand in greeting. Philip glanced curiously at Walter's companion, a stocky man, well past middle age, whose gray hair still showed golden streaks.

The man looked keenly at Philip before he reached out a hand. "My boy, you will never know the joy you gave me when I received your letter about my sister, whom I had thought to be dead all these years."

"Uncle John?" Philip said questioningly, the truth slowly dawning upon him that this was his mother's brother.

"Yes. I booked passage to America as soon as I could after your information arrived. How is she, son? Have the years been hard on her?"

Still grasping his uncle's hand, Philip answered, "No. No. Sometimes I think she grows more youthful. She will be glad you have come."

Walking to the house with his uncle, Walter having returned to Jamestown, Philip looked around for Towner; he was again working in the field.

Straightening from her work at the fireplace, Hayley had no trouble recognizing this man she had once considered her enemy.

"Master Lawrence," she said with all the graciousness of a queen. "Welcome to our home."

Hayley's dignity and poise was reminiscent of her role as Lady Grover. Without her evident pride, John might have pitied Hayley, but she gave no room for pity. John Lawrence didn't even compare her past to the simplicity of her home.

"I am eager to see my sister," John said as they finished the meal of venison, dried corn, and wheat bread that Hayley had prepared. "I must return to England on the vessel that brought me here."

"Should we bring Mum here or take him to see her?" Philip asked Hayley.

"Judging from my experience in traveling through these forests, he might not like any more walking." She flashed a look at John Lawrence. "Did you find the trip from Jamestown a bit wearing?" she asked, as he stifled a yawn.

"More than a 'bit', my dear, but I'm not a young man, you know."

"Then I shall go early in the morning to bring Mum here. We will return by nightfall."

When she saw Philip enter their clearing in late afternoon, with his mother close behind, Towaye was also with them. And the wise woman was wearing, not her blue silk dress, but her usual buckskin garments. She obviously was making a statement—though she possessed English clothing, she would not shame Towaye by seeming to be unhappy in her present situation.

She waited, but when John held out his arms and cried in a strained voice, "Sister," she ran to him.

Since John had to leave the next day, the reunited family talked long into the night. Towaye was quiet, and Lawrence made no particular overtures to him, but Hayley could not sense any tension between the two.

But when Maggie Lawrence related how Towaye had saved her life when the other Raleigh colonists had perished and when her conversation made it obvious that Towaye had brought happiness to her life, John directed

152

more than one grateful glance toward his brother-in-law. And the next day when he prepared to return to Jamestown, Lawrence reached for Towaye's hand.

"I have cause to be grateful to you, Towaye. Not only have you saved my sister's life, but you have helped her to retain faith in God. I will never cease to remember you in my prayers. It may be that we will not meet again upon this earth, but, please God, we will someday be united in Heaven."

Hayley watched Maggie carefully as Philip and John disappeared from view. No regret was mirrored in the blue eyes, and that fact gave Hayley courage. Even yet, she suffered lonely times, wondering if she would ever be sorry she had not returned to England.

With the tobacco curing in the barn, Hayley and Philip set out for Jamestown to visit the Johnsons. All summer Hayley had awaited further word from her uncle about his arrival with Roger, but she had heard nothing. Neither had Jacques Guise put in an appearance, and Hayley wondered if he'd intercepted her messages.

"Philip, if we don't see Guise at Jamestown, could you find out where he lives? I'm becoming anxious about Roger. In that letter, Uncle Simon indicated their arrival this summer. If they don't come soon, we needn't expect them until spring."

"Guise shouldn't be hard to locate. I know he lives somewhere on the edge of Jamestown, where the company is attempting to raise grapes. Being French, he was sent here to develop the wine industry. Although that enterprise is apparently a failure, he still stays on. I'll find him for you.

I want to have a few words with him anyway, for I'm sure the stories he spread about me prevented my election to the Burgesses."

"I declare," Paula protested in a tone that proved she was pleased at the way Philip and Hayley were fondling her offspring, "I do believe the two of you come here just to see Baby Walter. I don't receive any attention at all."

At first Philip had seemed afraid of the child, but as he became more accustomed to him, Hayley often handed Walter, Jr. to Philip. Seeing the way he played with the boy made her long to give him a child of his own.

If Paula noted any difference in the relationship of her two friends, she said nothing, but when she led them to her newly completed room where they would spend the night, Hayley was pleased that they could share those accommodations without embarrassment.

"We've had such terrible things happening the past few days," Paula gossiped as she hurried about to prepare the evening meal. "Indians attacked the settlers who went to Hog Island for some animals for the harvest feast. Then on Friday, a ship arrived from England, and the next day, one of the new arrivals was found lying wounded outside the stockade. He's near death now, it seems."

"Indians again?" Philip asked with slight interest. Such tragedies were common in Jamestown.

"Walter doesn't think so. The man had been bashed over the head with a heavy weapon . . . just didn't look like native work. Some thought when he arrived, he had a boy with him; but if he did, the boy is gone."

Philip looked quickly at Hayley and saw the color drain

from her face. He went to her side, but an imperative shake of her head assured him she was all right.

"Where is the wounded man?" he asked.

"Down in the guardhouse inside the fort."

In a few minutes, Philip made an excuse to leave them, and when he returned in a short time, he drew Hayley outside the house.

"I would have no way of knowing if it's your uncle, although without doubt, he did have a boy with him. He's unconscious, and I think he's dying."

"Shall we tell Paula?"

"No use, unless we know it is your uncle."

They hurried down the dusty street, Hayley's face fixed on the fort ahead of her. A bandage concealed most of the face contorted with pain, but it *was* Simon Douglas. Hayley dropped to her knees beside the pallet where he lay.

"Uncle Simon," she pleaded, disregarding any reason for secrecy now. "Where's Roger?"

The unconscious man stirred restlessly, and he murmured a few words, but Hayley could not understand. Philip brought water and bathed his face, and the guard helped them force some medicine into his mouth, but despite all their efforts, Simon Douglas died without regaining consciousness.

"Did he have any belongings?" Hayley asked the guard.

"A trunk, milady. It's at the home of Widow Smith."

Philip went back to Paula's house with Hayley before he made arrangements for Simon's burial. Deaths were frequent in Jamestown, and more than one burying ground had been started in the area.

Looking out toward the James River as the minister read

the burial service over Simon's grave, Hayley's thoughts were of Roger. It was too late to worry about Simon, but somewhere in this country, her son was in the hands of persons who wished him harm. She remembered the last time she'd seen her son—a small, proud boy dressed in the finest of silk garments and black leather boots, eagerly going to his first grown-up party. He had resisted his mother's kiss as she placed a chain around his neck bearing his own miniature that had been painted a few years before. Pausing at the door of her bedroom, however, he had run back to receive her caress, then he had bounded down the steps to the great hall to be captured by the king's men.

Remembering, Hayley sobbed, and Philip's strong arm supported her in more ways than one. She knew, even without him voicing the words, that he would find Roger for her.

After the short service, Philip stopped by the Widow Smith's to retrieve Simon's trunk. Hoisting the trunk on his shoulders, Philip carried it to the Johnsons'.

"If we may leave it here for a few weeks, then next time, I'll bring the cart or the shallop to transport it home."

Hayley's hands trembled as she opened the trunk and fingered the items of clothing. Philip turned away, unable to watch any longer the tears coursing down her face as she looked at the small doublets embroidered with the Grover coat-of-arms, silk shirts with lace collars, shiny leather boots, and woolen stockings.

Simon had packed a collection of Shakespeare's works, for many of the items in the trunk belonged to him, but Hayley looked wistfully at the few toys and books that she found. Hoping to find the miniature portrait of the boy, she searched the whole trunk, but the child's likeness was not included with the other items.

Hayley's tears had ceased by bedtime, but her body was tense in spite of Philip's comforting arms.

"Do you suppose Jacques Guise has taken him?" she asked. "He knew Uncle Simon was coming and that he was bringing Roger."

"How much do you know about Guise?"

"Nothing at all. I told you I hadn't heard of the man until Uncle Simon decided I should leave England and the only boat departing was on its way to America. I shudder to think what my life might have been if you hadn't found me."

"You aren't sorry then?" he asked, needing reassurance.

"Never! Surely you can tell that."

"I can tell it." His persuasive lips upon hers caused the past to recede.

Philip delayed their departure from Jamestown for another day, and in early morning, leaving Hayley at Paula's, he went to reconnoiter Guise's home. He hid in the forest and watched Guise and his sister, but there was no indication they had the boy. He even dared, after nightfall, to peer in their window. The boy wasn't at their home.

With a feeling of failure, he returned to Hayley.

"No news?"

"We'll find him, dearest. He has to be in the colony somewhere."

Philip was more gentle than ever on their way home. She had need of his strength that evening because when they entered their home, Hayley's eyes were drawn immediately to the table.

"Philip!" He turned from the fireplace, where he was kindling a flame. She held up an object she'd lifted from the table—a small portrait of a boy, but mutilated with a cross of red across the face.

"Roger?"

Hayley nodded, and in a shaking voice, she sobbed, "The last time I saw that it was around his neck. It was painted when he was five years old. What does this mean?"

"I don't know . . . I feel helpless, Hayley. I should be doing something, but I don't know where to turn. Will you allow me to discuss this with Father? He is wise; he may know what to do."

Hearing a sound at the door, they saw Towner standing there. Hayley slipped the miniature inside the pocket of her apron.

"Have you seen anyone here at the house?" Philip demanded harshly.

"No, sir. No one around 'cept me."

Philip stepped outside to discuss the farm work with Towner, and Hayley withdrew the picture and looked longingly at the face of her son. If no one had been around the plantation except Towner, had he placed the miniature on the table? Had he come from England to spy on her?

She was pacing the floor when Philip returned, and reading her thoughts, said, "Maybe he does know more than he pretends. I'm going to watch him."

"Saponi!" His noiseless approach startled Hayley.

He answered in Algonquian, and Hayley ignored him, going on with the hoeing she had been engaged in when he appeared. When he muttered again in guttural tones, she looked at him.

"You know I can't understand that. If you want to speak to me in English, I'll answer; otherwise, you're wasting my time."

"You are beautiful, Hayley. Why didn't I see you before Philip did? Always he gets what should have been mine."

"If you don't stop talking to me like that, I'm going to tell Philip, and what do you think he will do?"

"So you have not told him, and he is too blind to see for himself that you must be mine. He will do nothing. He's a Christian. He loves those who persecute him."

"And, you, Saponi, have you spurned the Christian teachings of your mother?"

He flung his arms wide in a vengeful gesture. "I hate the ways of the English. They must go."

"But your mother is English; I am English. Do you hate us?"

He turned away and would not answer. "Where is Philip? He was not in the field when I came by."

"He will return soon," she answered and continued to cut down the bean vines in her effort to prepare the soil for winter. Saponi leaned against the oak tree and watched her. When she glanced sideways, he was always staring at her, his eyes reminding her of Philip's when he made love to her.

With a feeling of relief, Hayley looked up to see Philip and Towner approaching the house, both laden with packs

159

of provisions for the winter. She left the garden enclosure when Philip came near, and he dropped his pack and took her into his arms.

"All right?" he whispered, and she nodded slightly as he released her. Before he greeted Saponi, he reached into his pack and brought out a block of sugar.

"The shopkeeper in Wolstenholme Towne said this had arrived only yesterday."

As meager as their finances were, he never went anywhere without bringing her a gift, and she kissed him softly on the cheek.

"Come inside, Saponi?"

The answer came in Algonquian.

"But why does he want to see me?" Philip questioned in English.

Saponi shrugged his shoulders.

"Who wants to see you?" Hayley asked quickly.

"Opechancanough." To Saponi, he said, "Well, I can't come right away. Do you want to stay the night?"

"No, I'm going to see Mum and Father before I return to the village."

"Does Opechancanough want to see them, too?"

"No, only you." He raised his hand in salute and disappeared into the forest as quickly as he had come.

chapter
11

PHILIP HADN'T TRAVELED MORE THAN a few miles into the forest before his need for Hayley cut at his inward being as a knife would tear a loaf of bread. He marveled that his life had become dependent upon her presence, and he smiled when he remembered their passionate farewell.

He shook his head in wonder when he considered that almost by accident, if one could consider God's will to be accidental, he had taken the granddaughter of a Scots queen to be his wife. He, who had longed to leave a rich heritage to his progeny, had ensured royal blood coursing through their veins.

Forcibly Philip pushed thoughts of Hayley from his mind to concentrate on the reason for his journey and his own safety as he plunged farther and farther into the dense forest. Perhaps he shouldn't have come alone, but he would not draw his father into trouble. He was also disturbed to leave Hayley by herself, although she had insisted that she was unafraid. And he had given Towner strict orders to stay away from the house.

Traveling due north to Opechancanough's village, he followed well-defined paths, and occasionally when he reached a higher elevation where he could look across the James Valley, he shook his head in dismay. At those times, he acknowledged the remaining strength of his Indian heritage, even though he had adopted European ways. The Algonquian in him mourned the loss of solitude, the days when a man could walk for many miles without seeing any sign of human habitation. As he saw the numerous farmsteads springing up along the James, he hurt for himself as well as for Towaye, who mourned these changes in his ancestral land.

Two days of hard walking brought him to Opechanca-nough's village. At this time of the year, the male Indians should have been out hunting for the winter season, but the town was crowded with warriors, and Philip noted that every one of them carried an English musket. *What has happened to the English law forbidding the sale of arms to the Indians?*

Philip presented himself at Opechancanough's lodge as soon as he arrived, for he wanted to conclude their interview and return home quickly. He didn't like the fact that Hayley was alone. She was more self-reliant than she had been at first, but he realized that she might have some reason for fearing Towner as well as those who would conspire to take her back to England. What would he do if he returned to find her gone? Had this summons to the Indian village been a ruse to secure his absence from the plantation? The thought brought chills to his body.

But Opechancanough would not see him; therefore, Philip looked for his brother. On his way to Saponi's lodge, a group of children, batting a ball, frolicked around the side of a building and ran into him. Philip laughed and stood aside, but his face sobered. Four English children were playing with the Indian youth in perfect contentment.

Saponi appeared at his side. "Where did you get the white children?" Philip demanded.

Saponi's face hardened. "Do you think we stole them?"

"There has to be some explanation. I'm asking for it."

Sarcastically, Saponi responded, "The great George Thorpe thought it would be a step toward the blending of our two cultures to make an exchange between some of our children and the English youth to learn the ways of each other. They have been here a few weeks."

"How many?"

Saponi held up six fingers.

"Where are the others?"

"Around. Nonna said to invite you to our lodge."

"I don't intend to stay long. I want to see Opechanca-nough and return home. It wasn't my idea to come here."

"You will see him when he decides to see you."

"If he doesn't see me by morning, I'll leave. I don't like to stay away from the plantation."

"Afraid to leave your English wife alone . . . afraid she will run away from you?"

"Afraid for her, yes, but not that she will run away. She is the only reason I came here to see if Opechancanough plans anything that will hurt her."

As they walked toward Saponi's lodge, Philip noted two other English children sitting apart from the others. One of these children, with long chestnut hair falling around his shoulders, drew Philip's attention, and he stopped.

Starting toward the two boys, he was detained when Saponi grasped his arm. "Leave them alone, Brother."

Philip was aware of the concern in his voice. In a lower tone, he added, "You are an enemy here." It had been a long time since Saponi had called him "Brother."

Philip glanced around; many armed warriors were watching their every move. "And you, too, Saponi. Am I your enemy?"

"As of now, you are still my brother. But the day is coming when that may not be so. Philip, the English must go."

"Why must they? George Thorpe doesn't have such a bad idea. Our two cultures can blend. Look at Mum and Father; witness my own marriage. We can live together peaceably, if both parties want it that way."

When they arrived at Saponi's lodge, Nonna set food before them, and they continued their conversation as they ate.

"Ah, but the English do not expect to change. They want us to be as they are. Tell me honestly, my brother, do you find the life of an English planter satisfying?"

"It has not been easy, for at first I was shunned by both English and Indian alike, but I've persevered, and most of the settlers accept me as an equal. Since I've had the fortune to marry an English woman, the path to the future should be secured. All prejudice may not be overcome in my lifetime, but my children will be upstanding citizens in this country."

Saponi shook his head in disagreement. "Your future is not secure, brother; do not plan for children that you do not have."

The comment disturbed Philip, but though he pressed Saponi for further explanation, he would say no more.

On into the night the two brothers conversed in a congenial manner that had not been their practice in recent years. Since they spoke in English, Nonna gave up trying to understand what they said and rolling into a bearskin, she went to sleep.

"But do you not miss the days of old, Philip?" Saponi asked once.

"The carefree days when we ran the forests for hours or harvested the corn with Mum and Father . . . yes, I miss them, Saponi, but they're gone! The English ruined that when they first came, but it had to be. Even Father agrees that our old way of life has gone forever. The English call it progress; they think we need their superior way of life. I will not agree that it is altogether superior, but it is the stronger culture, and it will survive."

Opechancanough summoned Philip early the next morning. Philip suppressed a smile when he entered the chieftain's presence. He sat on an elevated dias the English had given to Powhatan, his half-brother, and he wore a crimson robe that also had been a gift to Powhatan from the English. The only part of his appearance that suggested his Indian culture was the headdress of black feathers—a sign of war that Philip did not like.

Considering his obvious fondness for English furnishings, Opechancanough's first words were ironic. "The English must go."

"The English will *not* go, Opechancanough. You must accept the fact."

"The English will go, and you are to tell them so. They will listen to your counsel since you speak to them as an equal. You are to say to them that if they do not leave willingly, we will drive them out."

Philip did not answer for a moment, and his sympathy reached out to this man. He was the remnant of a passing race, and Philip recognized in him the same hopelessness he sometimes sensed in Towaye. Their old way of life was passing, and they could see no future for them.

Opechancanough's voice droned on, "The English have pushed too far inland. At first they were few, and the trees they hewed made only a slight scar on the landscape, but they continue to move farther and farther up the river. Soon we will be crowded to the mountains, and then where do we go? Our brothers west of the mountains do not want us. The Iroquois to the North are our enemies. Where do we go? There is no place left to run. Opechancanough says the days of running are over. We will fight and drive the English from our land."

Philip sensed that many other tribesmen had entered the lodge, but the silence was intense, broken only by a slight stir among those who listened.

"You may fight and drive a few English from the land, but that will not be the end of them. Their weapons are far superior to ours, and they will prevail. If you will not listen to me, at least heed the words of my father. He is wise, and he has been in the land of the English. He says they are more numerous than the fish of the sea. Their cities are crowded with people awaiting passage to these shores. They prize land as a possession."

"But it is our land they prize."

Philip spread wide his hands. "In whose opinion? I'm not saying which is right or wrong; I'm only explaining the inevitable. To survive, I have chosen to become English, for there is no way to stop the Europeans. Already to the north of us in the land of the Huron, the French are moving in. Northeast, a small band of English have taken root. To the South and West the Spanish have occupied the land. There is no stopping the Europeans," Philip repeated.

Opechancanough stood to his full height, and on the uplifted dias, he made a formidable figure. He avoided Philip's reasoning, declaring in a sonorous voice, "I have summoned you, Philip Lawrence, to tell the English to leave. If not, they will suffer."

"Sending such a message is useless, and I will not deliver it. You may strike at the English, but they will retaliate. You are inviting the death of your people."

"And have you forgotten that I once gave succor to your family when you had no place to go?" The chief's eyes beheld Philip with piercing intensity, and Philip stared at him, his eyes unwavering, not wanting the Indian to think he was intimidated. "And you, Philip Lawrence, where do you stand? Are you for us or against us?"

The decision had been made long ago as far as Philip was concerned, but he chose his words carefully. He had his mother as well as Hayley to consider. "It is my opinion that the best way for the English and the Algonquians to survive is to live as brothers. It can be done."

Opechancanough spat scornfully. "It cannot be done. When the salt water of the ocean flows into the big river, our stream is polluted. The two cannot mix and produce pure water. So it is with the English. They have polluted our way of life. The two will not mix." His voice thundered through the room, "Are you for us or against us?"

"The blood of an English mother flows through my veins; my wife is English; her children will be English. My choice is made."

Opechancanough drew a hatchet from his belt and threw it toward Philip. He did not dodge as the deadly weapon hurtled his way. Standing with a serenity he did not feel, when the hatchet was a few feet from his chest, he reached out and grabbed it with his right hand. Deliberately, he tossed the weapon back to Opechancanough, where it came to rest in the earthen floor at his feet. A flicker of surprise filtered over the chief's face.

"You are a brave man, Philip Lawrence. It is a pity you have chosen the wrong side, for you will die with the other English. Do not count on any English children. Dead women do not bear infants."

He indicated the conclusion of the interview, and with a feeling of relief he did not reveal, Philip turned his back on the chieftain. As he neared the door, Philip saw Saponi standing by the wall. He paused in his stride, and the two brothers stared at each other. Philip reached out his hand, and for a moment he thought Saponi would take it, but with a show of contempt, Saponi spat at his brother's feet and turned his back on him.

The musket in his hand gave Philip no sense of security as he walked from the village watched by hundreds of unfriendly eyes. He knew he wouldn't use the musket, thereby taking a chance of not returning to Hayley. He again saw the English boy, who seemed so unhappy with his surroundings, and when the child stared beseechingly at Philip, he stopped to talk to him, but two armed warriors nudged him out of the village with muskets at his back.

Despite his need and urgency to return to Hayley, Philip decided he must reroute his journey and stop at Henrico to see George Thorpe. Although he didn't intend to tell all Opechancanough had said, he thought he should give a mild warning to the English, even though it would make his journey longer.

Philip and Thorpe had become good friends during the days he had worked on the college buildings, and Thorpe greeted Philip with warmth.

"And how is your lovely wife?" he asked at once. "I have planned to stop by to hear her play the lute once again, but we have been so busy here."

"She is well," Philip answered. "I was nearby, and I wanted to check on your progress." Philip had noted much work had been accomplished on the Indian school since the days he had spent here a few months before.

Thorpe was still enthusiastic in his praise of the project. "We hope to begin our studies in the spring. Communications have come from England that teachers will be arriving next summer. Already we have started our student exchange system. We have some Indian boys studying with us, and five of our youth are living happily in Opechancanough's village."

"Five?" And at Thorpe's nod, Philip thought again of the children he'd seen. Saponi had said six, and Philip was sure he'd counted six different boys.

As Thorpe led Philip around the streets of the town, a languid hound followed at their heels. "What has happened to your mastiffs?" Philip asked.

With a wave of his hand, Thorpe answered. "I had to have the beasts killed. They scared the natives, whom I wanted to feel at ease in our town."

The Indians certainly did feel at ease, Philip noted. Twenty or more natives filtered in and out of the settlers' houses as freely as the English did themselves.

Thorpe enthusiastically praised Opechancanough. "A goodly man," he said, "and one willing to have the best for his people. We have had many good visits when he has come to Henrico." He pointed to the house he had built for the Indian chief. "He has taken on our culture and seems content to dwell with us."

"But have you ever considered that Opechancanough's friendliness could be false and that the Indians aren't happy about the English encroachment on their lands? The settlers may be in danger of attack."

"My boy," the kindly Thorpe said, placing a beefy hand on Philip's broad shoulders. "You must be mistaken. We have had little Indian trouble here for several years; the halcyon days are here to stay."

All the way home Philip thought of the beaming expression on Thorpe's face. He felt defeated by the man's optimism and expectation.

Walking grimly through the forest and feeling the need to see Hayley pierce his mind and body, Philip could not forget the extra child at the village. *Why did those eyes haunt him?*

Not until he was almost home did he admit what he knew must be the truth. Roger was in the hands of Opechancanough, and if the chief knew the boy belonged to Hayley, he would try to use Roger's safety to force Philip to join him. Why hadn't he threatened to harm Roger? Was it possible the chief didn't know the child's identity?

Guided by a brilliant moon, Philip walked long after midnight. He was tired, but his need to see Hayley overcame his natural fatigue.

The house was dark when he entered the clearing, but that didn't alarm Philip, for Hayley wouldn't have expected him tonight. He paused for a moment and looked with pride at the home he'd carved from the wilderness, and for a moment, he didn't see the small house made of half-timber and clay, with a thatched roof. He envisioned Haywood! He'd seen pictures of large English houses in the books Hayley had found in her uncle's trunk. Someday a similar house would rise on this spot.

Not wanting to startle Hayley, Philip called to her through the door before he knocked. "I'm home, Hayley. It's Philip. Come, open the door."

He heard her sleepy cry—a sound of welcome that warmed his heart. Her slight footsteps raced toward the door, she lifted the latchstring, and in a moment, he gathered her into his arms, drawing strength from the slender body he felt through the thin shift she wore.

"Oh, you're cold, Philip," she murmured when the chill from his buckskin jacket caused a tremor to course through her body. But when he started to release her, she melted more firmly into his embrace. "Oh, don't let me go. I've missed you so much."

His laugh was tremulous with emotion. "At least let me close the door. I've missed you, too, love-of-my-life."

She helped him out of his coat and turned to stir up the fire. "Do you want something to eat, Philip. I made fresh bread today, hoping that you would come."

"I'm hungry, yes, but not as much as I hunger for you. I

171

can't bear being separated from you." In the dim light from the fire she'd kindled, Philip stared intently at her, his eyes following every feature as she returned his gaze. The few flecks of green weren't visible, but he knew they were there. The oval mouth was inviting his kisses, and the long chestnut hair flowed freely over his arms. He groaned inwardly when he thought of what the future might hold for them, but he sought her lips with his, and they shared love at its sweetest.

She withdrew a bit from the circle of his arms. "What did Opechancanough want, Philip?"

"Let me sleep now, Hayley. We'll talk in the morning."

Hayley was out of bed and prepared his breakfast before Philip awakened. She sat on the side of the bed and pressed a soft kiss on his forehead until he opened his eyes.

"Sleepyhead," she chided lovingly.

"I was in such a hurry to return to you that I only took two short naps. Hayley, the news isn't good."

"I feared as much," she said as she placed porridge on the table. After Philip refreshed himself with the warm water she provided, he ate ravenously of the food she gave him. Satisfied, he pulled her down on his knees.

"Hayley, I want you to return to England." He had thought it all out on his way home.

"Why?" Her face paled, and she tried to rise from his knees, but he held her.

"It's just for a while, dearest. There's war coming, and England is the only safety I can envision for you."

"But you know Uncle Simon thought I was in danger there, too."

"Don't you have some family in France? Maybe you could go there, and I wish Mum would go with you."

"But what have you learned, Philip?"

"Opechancanough's village is an armed camp, but he's lulled the English into thinking he's their friend. He tried to force me into telling them to get out, and when I refused, he made me declare myself either for or against him. Of course, I could make only one choice."

"Then you're in just as much danger as I. I won't leave you."

"Can you give me one good reason you shouldn't choose the safety of England over possible death here?"

"Do you want your son to be born in England?" she said directly.

Philip stared at her blankly, not comprehending at first the import of her words. His hands tightened on her waist. "You're sure," he whispered, and he ran his hands lightly over her stomach.

"Yes, I'm sure," she said. "You know this isn't the first time I've borne a child, and I'm sure. Your child is going to be born right here."

"And how do you know it will be a son?" His voice was muffled.

She ran her fingers through her thick hair which had come untied from the wide band. "I can't guarantee *that*, but we have a fifty-fifty chance. Well, is my reason good enough to convince you I should stay with you?"

He raised his head at last and kissed her. "You stay. Whatever happens, we'll see it through together. I didn't know how I could possibly live without you, but for your safety, I was willing to try. I don't think Opechancanough will strike this winter, but we will be on guard anyway."

Philip delayed his departure from the house until Hayley went to milk the goats. He opened the top drawer of the chest where she kept her belongings and rummaged carefully until he found the miniature of her son. Although the visage had been marred, the features were still recognizable, and comparison of this face to that of the unhappy European child in the Indian village left no doubt in Philip's mind. Hayley's son was a prisoner of Opechancanough. But nothing should mar her evident happiness about the birth of their child.

chapter 12

Spring 1622

HAYLEY MONITORED THE PROGRESS OF WINTER by the changes in her body. By January the movement and growth of the child were often apparent, reminding her of seven years earlier, when she had been awaiting her firstborn. Fear for Roger depressed her, and she crept around the house until Philip finally determined what was bothering her.

"Dearest," he began one night when he was brushing her hair. "I hadn't decided what to do about this, but when you told me that you were going to bear our child, I thought you would be as well off not to know." He paused. "Now, I feel I must tell you. I'm sure I saw Roger in Opechancanough's camp when I was there last fall."

"Oh, Philip," Hayley said reproachfully, "it is sure that you do not understand a mother's heart. But I will not blame you, for you thought you were doing the right thing. Tell me, did he seem well?"

"I had only a glimpse of the boy a couple of times, and I was unable to talk to him. It wasn't until I was on the journey home that I realized his hair was much like yours, although he didn't look like you otherwise."

"No, the child always favored the Grovers, rather than my family."

"And unlike the other English children there, he seemed sad."

"I miss him so! Is there no possible way we can rescue him?"

"I've thought about it all winter. I didn't want to risk leaving you here when I could be taken prisoner, or killed, if I went back to Opechancanough's village. It's been such a worry to me that I should have shared it with you sooner. To gain one son, you might have lost this new life growing within you. Life's decisions are never easy, Hayley."

"He's alive! Come spring, we will think of some way to bring him home."

"And spring may soon be upon us, dearest, and after the long winter, it will be welcome. I heard a bluebird singing today, and a few leaves are appearing on the willows along the river bank."

By the middle of March Hayley could see signs of spring from the doorway. One tree was showing a few white blossoms, and from the house, the green on the willows at the river was visible. Hayley breathed deeply of the fresh air before she turned back inside. Her hand caressed her stomach where an unmistakable small foot pushed against her flesh.

Supper was nearly ready when a knock at the door aroused Hayley. Now that her body was becoming heavier, she often dozed a bit before Philip came in for the night. The knock disturbed her, for visitors were rare and never came at this hour of the night. Perhaps she had pulled the latchstring inside and had barred Philip from the house, for sometimes she secured the door to prevent Towner's entering.

"Saponi! Nonna!" Hayley said, surprised. "Come in." Saponi entered the room first, and Nonna pushed a child after him—a child who had been standing behind Nonna when Hayley opened the door.

Comprehension slowly entered Hayley's mind. "Roger!" she exclaimed as she gathered her child into her arms. Tears threatened to overflow when she looked into the tiny face that had haunted her dreams for over two years.

"Mum?" he said cautiously. "I thought I was never to see you again."

Hayley glanced up at Saponi and was surprised to see a strange look in his eyes. *Sadness or shame?* Which was the emotion that covered his face? But why would he express sadness now when he had made her happy? Still holding the child, she grabbed the table to help raise her heavy body from the floor.

"Thank you, Saponi, Nonna. My heart has ached for the sight of the boy."

Entering the house, Philip stopped short at the sight of visitors.

"Philip," Hayley cried, "look who has come to live with us." Then, fearfully, she pulled Roger close to her and looked suspiciously at Saponi. "You don't intend to take him away again, do you? How do you happen to have him in the first place?"

Saponi didn't answer her first question, saying instead, "He was brought to the village when I was away. That's all I know."

"Will you spend the night with us? It's late now," Hayley asked as she placed food on the table.

With a slight nod, Saponi accepted the invitation. When Philip left the house for some more wood for the fire, Saponi looked pointedly at Hayley's bulging stomach. "I see you no longer sleep alone."

The atmosphere in the room during the evening seemed more strained than usual, although Hayley had never been able to converse with Nonna, and the question of the former relationship between her and Philip remained.

When Philip reached for the Bible for the nightly reading, Saponi turned his back and appeared not to listen. Philip read from the book of Matthew, and Hayley wondered if he had deliberately chosen the passage. "Put up again thy sword into his place: for all they that take the sword shall perish with the sword." Saponi's back seemed to become more rigid as Philip read.

After Nonna and Saponi had gone to their bed in the loft, Philip drew Roger toward him. "Son, do you think you could like being a Virginia planter? Your mother and I welcome you here to live with us."

He stood very erect for such a small child, and Hayley marveled that he had been able to retain the Grover pride and dignity during the trying circumstances he'd endured. The loss of his father, his grandfather, and the uncle who had tried to protect him was enough to ruin his life, even without having being separated from her for so long, but she vowed to herself that she would make it up to him someday.

They made a bed for Roger near the fire, and when the candle was extinguished, and they were in bed, Hayley snuggled close to Philip. She thought her happiness had reached its zenith. She had everything she wanted—Roger safe, Philip by her side, and a new Lawrence on its way.

Eventually the thought that Philip was not as happy as she filtered its way into her mental rejoicing. *Did he resent Roger?* Surely he wouldn't mind having the boy live with them when he'd assured her that he would love Roger as his own.

"What's troubling you, Philip?" she whispered at last.

"Something is wrong, dearest. I don't know what, but all this doesn't ring true to me."

"Why, what do you mean?" she said, her voice rising.

He placed a tender hand over her mouth in a bid for quietness.

"Why did they bring him back now? Nonna has never spent a night in our house, or Father's. Why did they stay here tonight?"

"Surely your suspicions are unjust; they seemed friendly enough."

"Too friendly. Remember, I've known Saponi all my life. I can usually tell when he's being evasive."

Philip's doubts left Hayley restless, and unable to find a comfortable position, she twisted from her right side to her left and then tried to lie on her back. Philip's rigid body beside her confirmed that he did not sleep either. Languid from lack of sleep, Hayley pulled out of bed the next morning. Perhaps if she'd feed their guests, they would be on their way.

Kneeling beside Roger's pallet, she rubbed his curly locks. Except for his hair, she could see nothing of herself in him; he was all Grover if looks were an indicator.

After breakfast, Philip reluctantly rose to go outside to perform the morning chores, which he had taken over in the past few months to spare Hayley the work. Unable to converse with Nonna, Hayley tried to carry on a conversation with Saponi, for the quietness in the room was making her nervous. His attention was not on what she was saying, for he rose and went to the window, as if to assure himself of Philip's whereabouts. When he turned from the window, Nonna moved to stand behind Hayley, who, intercepting Saponi's signal, tried to rise. She was grabbed from behind in an iron grasp and forced to sit down as Nonna's hand covered her mouth.

Seeing the attack on his mother, Roger ran to help, but Saponi covered the space between them in one jump. As he grabbed the boy, his arm lifted in an arc, and the knife that had appeared in his hand, sank deep into Roger's back. Inwardly, Hayley screamed as her son groaned and with sightless eyes slumped to the floor. She turned tortured eyes toward Saponi, who refused to meet her gaze but quietly went to the fireplace and took a cloth from the shelf.

Struggling for freedom, Hayley bit Nonna's hand, thinking that would loosen her grip but the strong woman drew Hayley's head backward into a stranglehold. Blackness engulfed her, and she knew no more.

When Hayley regained consciousness, her hands were tied with a deerskin thong, and a cloth was fastened in her mouth. Saponi was standing beside the door with Philip's musket in his hands. Recognizing Philip's step, Hayley prayed for some way to warn him, but Nonna's grip prevented her from moving before Philip opened the door.

Sensing danger, Philip jumped to attack Saponi, but he was too late. The musket discharged, and Philip tumbled to the floor. Hayley wondered if she would be next, but Saponi grabbed her by the hand and pulled her to the door, forcing her to step over Philip's bloody body. Dry-eyed, Hayley watched as Nonna took coals from the fireplace and scattered them throughout the room. They had destroyed the people who meant most to her. Now were they going to destroy everything material she and Philip had worked for? In the barnyard, Nonna and Saponi killed the goats and the chickens, and torched the buildings.

"Towner," Saponi muttered to Nonna, and she moved toward the farm buildings. Shoving Hayley before him, Saponi moved quickly into the forest.

Surely she would awaken soon to learn that this was all a bad dream. But as she stumbled along, and the miles receded behind them, she had to admit the bitter truth. Roger and Philip were both dead, and everything they had was destroyed. Was she going to end her days here in Virginia as she had started out? Husband and child gone, and herself near death. She didn't want to live now. Still, as she felt the child heavy upon her body, she knew she had that life to preserve. But what life would the child have without a father, and herself a prisoner of her enemies?

As they traveled along the river, Hayley saw many spirals of smoke drifting upward in the cool morning air, generating the thought that the attack upon them hadn't been an isolated incident. Was Opechancanough making good his threat to drive the English out of Virginia?

Hayley was cold, and the burden of the child was causing her to gasp for each breath. At last, she could take no more, and she stopped, leaning against a pine tree. Saponi prodded her in the back, but she refused to budge and sat down on the cold ground.

"Move! We will rest later." She shook her head, looked pleadingly at him, and he dropped beside her to untie her hands and to loosen the gag from her mouth.

Rubbing her arms to bring back the feeling, she glanced quickly at him, but he turned his back on her and would not meet her eyes.

"Why, Saponi? Your own brother?"

"He was not my brother. He had made his choice."

She knew it was futile to argue that point with him. "Then, kill me, too. You've taken all that I love. I have nothing to live for."

"You have the child. It will be ours. If not for this child, you would have perished with Philip."

"Saponi, you're not serious. You hate the rest of the English. Why not me?" His eyes, full of restrained passion, gave her his answer—he had coveted her from the first moment he had seen her.

Hayley knew she must watch her tongue, for she sensed the savage quality controlling this man. "From now on, the English will bother us no more." He waved his arm broadly. "You see the fires. Many plantations and towns are wasted. Opechancanough has struck in all points. The English are gone . . . dead."

"Your mother, too?" Hayley breathed fearfully.

He dropped his head shamefully, and for many minutes he did not speak. During that silence, Hayley became aware of the stillness—the pall of death—hanging over the whole area.

"I persuaded my father to take her to Jamestown. To my shame, Hayley, I was not true Indian to the core. In the end, I could not take her life. I doubted that Opechancanough would have her harmed, for she has been good to his people, but I wanted to be sure."

"But why did Towaye not come to warn Philip?"

"I told him I would bring the message to him." And so, trusting the word of their son, Towaye and Maggie Lawrence had left Philip and Hayley to their enemies.

"Did you kill Philip so you could take me?"

Saponi squatted beside her. "Philip angered Opechancanough, and he decreed his death. The chief has planned this for many years. He has befriended the whites to keep them from knowing his plans. The Indians were not suspected; they came and went among their white friends without problem. At the appointed time this morning, we struck in many places. Opechancanough sent the boy back to you so that you would not become suspicious of our visit."

"But how did Opechancanough capture Roger? Tell me."

"Your servant brought the boy to the village."

"Towner?"

Saponi nodded. "Told the chief he would pay big reward if he held the boy until Towner came again. Opechancanough waits for no one. Used the boy for his own purposes."

Searching for a reason Towner would capture Roger, Hayley didn't protest when Saponi pulled her upward and urged her to continue along the trail. She remembered the time she'd left England thinking she would never know happiness again. She had found Philip and his love, and perhaps even yet, through their child, she could keep his memory alive.

Nightfall covered them when they were far north of the plantation. The wind had been cold all day, but the sun had shone, giving Hayley some knowledge of the direction they traveled.

When Saponi started a fire, Hayley eased down wearily beside its warmth. Her feet were swollen until her ankles bulged over the heavy boots she had fortunately put on this morning.

No food was available, but Saponi piled some dried leaves for Hayley to rest on. Closing her eyes, she remembered the time she'd traveled from Jamestown with Philip. A sound aroused her, and she opened her eyes. Saponi lay crumpled up beside her. Jacques Guise and Towner stood over him.

Holding on to a tree, Hayley struggled to her feet.

"Let's get out of here," Guise muttered. "More Indians may be around. We're foolish to risk our necks out here when these natives are on the warpath."

"True," Towner responded, "but I was too near to accomplishing my mission to have it snatched away from me."

"You've come to save me?" Hayley asked Guise.

But Towner answered her, "Yes, milady. You're too valuable to become an Indian's harlot."

In spite of the cold, Hayley felt the blood rush to her face.

"The *Phantom* leaves Jamestown in two days. We'll be on her. Did you think such a notorious figure as yourself could just disappear from sight? I left England searching for you; it was good fortune that Master Lawrence needed a strong hand. 'Twas handy to keep my eye on you."

"But who are you?" Hayley asked, her mind struggling to remember this man.

"Once the heavy foliage is removed," he said, fingering his black whiskers, "you might recognize me as Arnold Wright, your father's coachman. You might also remember that you resented my slight advances toward you when you were a great lady, you had no time for the lowly coachman, but in this country, you marry a savage."

"Aren't you the one who betrayed our plot to the king?"

He bowed mockingly, paying no heed to Guise's pleas to hurry away. Guise was peering anxiously into the black forest, obviously terrified.

Towner bowed mockingly again. "I have the honor."

Again, Hayley remembered seeing him at the wharf when the *Jonathan* had sailed, so it had been easy for him to learn her whereabouts.

He pushed her before him. "Come along now. You'll be worth a pretty sum to me when I deliver you to England."

"But how did you escape from Nonna this morning?" Hayley asked as she started limping along the trail.

"I saw what was happening at the big house and escaped into the forest."

"Did you check on Philip?"

"He's gone where all good Indians should go."

The next few hours were exhausting to Hayley. Once, unbidden, she stopped to rest, and she said to Guise who was nearby, "And where do you come into this?"

185

"I am a poor man, cousin. I must answer when opportunity calls. The wine industry, it has not produced well for the London Company, so income has been meager. Thus, I accept a small commission from Towner. Too bad, however, for the death of the child. Two more valuable than one."

Would she find no end to her anguish? What other blows could life deal? But despite the suffering she was enduring, her heart ached also for her mother-in-law— both sons gone, and in such a tragic manner.

Suddenly Guise, who was walking behind Hayley, emitted an animal-like grunt, and hearing a thud behind her, Hayley turned quickly to see Guise falling to the ground. Saponi stood weaving behind him, a bloody knife in his hand. Towner turned at the sound, and lifting his musket, blasted Saponi as the latter jumped forward to sink the knife into Towner's throat.

Hot saliva welled up into Hayley's mouth and she retched. She had had nothing to eat since morning and vomited until she collapsed on the ground.

Head swimming, hand on her stomach where her child stirred in protest, Hayley leaned against a tree and surveyed the scene. Three men lay on the ground, but only Saponi seemed to be alive. Rising on an elbow, he beckoned to her. She crawled to his side, ignoring the blood welling from his breast.

"You must flee to Jamestown," he muttered weakly. "It may be that the residents there were able to withstand Opechancanough's attack. Find our mother; she will care for you."

"But which way, Saponi? I'm not sure I can find my way through the forest."

He motioned weakly to the left. "The river is there, a short ways." He coughed, and Hayley feared he was dying. "Follow river. Take longer, but you can't get lost. Keep river in sight."

Disregarding her safety, Hayley wouldn't leave Saponi as long as he lived. She sat by his side, holding his hand. After all, he was Philip's brother, and at the end, he had saved her life. For a long time, it seemed, he lay quietly, his breathing forced. At daybreak, he roused again, and his eyes were lucid for a moment. "He *was* my brother. I loved him."

When he breathed his last, Hayley left the spot quickly. She would have preferred to bury Saponi, but already the child within her was protesting the rough night they'd endured. She couldn't end that life with the effort it would have taken to bury Saponi.

chapter
13

SEVERAL HOURS PASSED before Hayley came to a path that paralleled the river, where she noted the flow of the water and headed toward Jamestown. Before long she arrived at an unfamiliar village, where smoldering buildings and several corpses witnessed to the ravishment. Anyone spared in the attack had apparently fled to safety elsewhere.

She hurried by the settlement, but when she came to a destroyed farmsite, she pillaged for food. A hen scurried off a nest in a small building that had only partly burned. Breaking the two eggs she found, and holding her nose, Hayley closed her eyes and swallowed the contents of the shells. Inside an earthen cellar, she discovered some potatoes and carrots, which she stored in her apron pockets, nibbling on the unpeeled, dirty vegetables as she walked along.

Staying alert, for fear she would encounter hostile natives, she hoped instead that she would find some settler to help her. She especially kept an eye out for Nonna, wondering why the girl hadn't followed Saponi.

Hayley's progress was slow because of the shifting weight of her child, and she had covered very few miles by late afternoon. As the day lengthened, she began to doubt the wisdom of remaining on the trail, reasoning it was a path the natives normally used. Still, straying from the marked route wasn't practical either, for if she went closer to the river, she sank into marshland. Venturing into the forest could cause her to lose the way, although by nightfall, she had no clear idea in what direction she was going. A mist started in late evening, and before dusk, a steady drizzle was making her miserable.

Shivering from the cold, her body suffering from fatigue, Hayley tried to stifle the sob that rose to her throat. Why was she putting forth such effort? The future was pointless, uncertain. What reason did she have for living?

Once she paused on the steep bank of the James, now at its fullest because of the high tide. How easy it would be to end it all! She was tempted, but in a moment of indecision, her babe twisted convulsively, and Hayley grabbed her abdomen in contrition. No, he deserved a chance in life! And she turned toward the hill, determined to find some shelter for the night.

Her clothes were soaked, and her hair hung in strings over her face. Believing her feet couldn't carry her farther, she somehow found the strength to stumble on. She eventually came to a ruined farmstead perched on a knoll overlooking the river. Standing quietly in the forest, peering intently into the clearing, Hayley could see no sign of life. The house had been burned, and a few dead animals littered a walled enclosure near the dwelling.

She ventured cautiously into the exposed area. A settler and two women lay dead, their bodies mutilated horribly. Hayley turned away quickly, but she retained her composure. After what she'd experienced today, her well of compassion was drained, but she shrieked when she was nudged from behind. A nanny goat bleated a welcome, and a smile touched Hayley's lips. How wonderful to see *anything* alive. She had been wondering if she and one chicken were the only living creatures in the colony of Virginia. And the goat's udder bulged with milk—another reason to be grateful.

Daylight was waning, and Hayley looked in desperation for some kind of container. An earthen jar lay in the ruins of the burned house, and moving as quickly as her cumbersome body would allow, Hayley grabbed the jar and placed it under the goat's udder. The warm milk hissing along the side of the container reminded Hayley of their plantation, and she fought back tears as she recalled the happy days she'd shared with Philip. *No need to mourn, just be thankful you had him even for a short while.* She produced enough milk to take care of her evening meal, with some left for breakfast, but before she drank, she searched for shelter.

Happening upon a cellar dug behind the dwelling, Hayley slipped guardedly down the steps into the cavern. After a few moments, her eyes adjusted to the darkness, enabling her to see that she was in a small room, filled with the aromatic scent of herbs and vegetables. A wooden bench along the wall held several jars, but pushing them to one side, Hayley eased her weary body onto the low bench.

Only then did she give way to tears. Why had she been left behind when all her loved ones were gone? Again she was reminded by the active child in her womb that she wasn't alone. She thought of Maggie Lawrence and

Towaye, who had lost both sons; if they still lived, at least she could give them a grandchild.

But how was she going to manage? The plantation had been destroyed, and she couldn't run it by herself. She supposed she could go back to England and claim the Douglas lands, which were hers now, but she had already given her loyalty to the New World. Besides, Philip would want his son reared in America. Strange that she hadn't doubted the child would be a boy.

The room was soon plunged into complete darkness, and Hayley stretched her bloated body on the narrow bench. Finally, when she ceased her inner and physical strife, and allowed her mind to rest, God spoke to her through the psalmist. "I will say of the Lord, he is my refuge and my fortress: my God, in him will I trust."

What an humbling thought! After the way God had guided and protected her during the past three years, why did she think her personal welfare was *her* concern only? Hayley had thought she knew the meaning of that promise before, but not until today had she experienced God's sheltering arms to the fullest. Always before, someone else had helped her—Uncle Simon, Paula, Philip. A dismal day of wandering through Virginia's wilderness was necessary to reassure Hayley that God had been her protector all of her life.

That sleepless night, which might otherwise have been a time of fear, brought peace to Hayley's troubled mind. She made a new commitment of her life to God. The glitter and security of the past—the throne of England, the Grover and Douglas riches, Roger, Philip, the plantation—were gone. "Lovest thou me more than these?" Jesus had asked the Apostle Peter. She asked herself the same question now.

Before morning came, she replied in the affirmative. "Yes, Lord, I love you above all else. I don't understand why the past had to be wiped clean, but I realize I'm alive for some purpose."

When the light of day evicted darkness from her sanctuary, Hayley heard steps above her. Should she call out? Was help nearby? She sat quietly, breathless, behind her fortress, as the sound of moccasined feet receded into the distance. Hayley waited a long while before she made a move, and when she stood, she doubled with pain as her child twisted violently and moved into a head-down position.

"Bring some help, God," she whispered. "This child is coming."

She stumbled up the stairs, her hand caressing her gyrating stomach. Despite the intermittent pain of beginning labor, she remembered to look around cautiously before she stepped into the sunlight.

Although the carnage of death surrounded her, she sensed the imminence of spring. Thankful for the sunny day, Hayley determined her position and headed westward along the river. If the sun shone all day, she could keep her bearings toward Jamestown; however, heavy clouds rolled in, and Hayley lost all sense of direction.

She plodded, avoiding rough spots, unthinking, intent on making one foot follow the other. If the labor pains became too severe, she leaned against a tree and gasped for breath, instead of dropping to the ground and experiencing the struggle of rising.

All signs indicated that her child would be born before morning. Did she remember enough about Roger's birth to perform the necessary services? For the arrival of her firstborn, she had been surrounded by midwives and nuns to ensure the safe arrival of the Grover heir.

Wearied from exertion and the pain that wrenched her body, Hayley had been oblivious to her surroundings for several hours; thus, without warning, she walked into a familiar clearing. Her feet halted of their own volition. In spite of the cold wind from the James, sweat broke out on Hayley's body, and she held on to a tree to support her quaking limbs.

She had come home.

The house was reduced to ashes. Wild animals had mutilated the bodies of their domestic stock. Intuition told her to flee, rather than to wallow in memories, but her feet refused to do her bidding. She circled the building site, trying to spot the remains of her loved ones, but no trace of them could be seen.

Glancing riverward, she was surprised to see their barn still standing. Apparently Nonna had not completed the work Saponi had sent her to do. Hayley wended her way slowly toward the barn, thankful she would at least have shelter for the birth of her child.

Her hand flew to her throat when she observed a small mound along the path. A grave? She knew it hadn't been here a few days ago. Could Roger be buried there? But who would have rescued his body from the burning building? Perhaps Towner had buried the boy before he accompanied Guise to intercept her. If Roger, why not Philip? She looked around the clearing but saw no evidence of another grave.

Sensing she wasn't alone, Hayley looked up quickly. Nonna stood directly before her, barring her path to the barn.

Had she struggled for two days only to meet her death at the hand of this woman? Hayley pivoted on sore feet and started to run, but Nonna overtook her easily. Terror-stricken when strong arms grabbed her from behind, Hayley turned fiercely on the Indian woman, flailing her enemy with quivering hands. "Let me go. Have you no mercy on anyone? Let me go."

Nonna shook her head and pulled Hayley toward the river. Hayley dug her heels into the damp soil to impede their progress, but her struggles ceased when her lower extremities were flooded with warm liquid, and she slumped into Nonna's waiting arms.

Hayley's head reeled, and she tried to sit up, but determined hands forced her backward. The ground beneath her was dry, and she sensed the familiar odor of dried tobacco leaves. Around her were piled some cloths and furs that Philip had used to cover the tobacco, so she knew she had reached the shelter of the barn.

A sliver of moonlight shifting through the logs illuminated Nonna's oblique features as the Indian woman leaned over her. Hayley tried to rise, fear coursing through her body.

"No," Nonna muttered in broken English. "I help. Save Philip's baby."

Hayley's floundering ceased. Was this girl to be her deliverer? Or was she concerned only with Philip's child? Once the baby arrived, would Nonna destroy her and take the child? But she had no choice, Hayley realized as she doubled her knees and writhed on the dirt floor.

Perhaps it was the hardship of the past few days, but the delivery seemed much more difficult than she remembered. During the night, she was thankful for Nonna's tender, skillful hands.

And when the pain seemed unbearable, Hayley had an overwhelming sensation of Philip's presence, as if he were holding her hand, embracing her, whispering, "I love you, dearest one," as he had so often in the hours between darkness and dawn.

The gray of the morning was seeping through the cracks of the barn when Hayley, gasping and exhausted, heard the lusty cry of her newborn. Sleep was claiming her, but she had to know.

"Boy or girl?"

Nonna held the unwashed child close to her face. *A girl!* So that ended Philip's hopes for a Lawrence dynasty in America. His dreams for Haywood were doomed. Why did she have to fail him?

Hayley awakened to a nuzzling mouth seeking her breast, and dreamily she looked at the small body Nonna held against her. Wrapped in a scrap of clean cloth, the mite of humanity looked at its new world through bleary blue eyes—Philip's eyes—but a chestnut fuzz colored the baby's head. *So this child will also resemble the great Mary, Queen of Scots.* Hayley hugged her daughter; she had always dreamed of bearing a girl child.

"Thank you, Nonna. She's all I have left."

An expression almost like a smile flitted across Nonna's dour face, and she shook her head.

Hayley looked where Nonna gestured, and a shriek escaped her lips. Philip! Just a few feet from where she lay, her beloved husband reclined on a pallet of furs. Blue eyes smiled at her from a fever-ravaged face, and he extended a trembling hand.

"Oh, Philip!" she said, and her lips quivered. "No wonder I sensed your presence last night." She crawled across the cold floor and took his hand.

"Afraid I wasn't much help to you. I've been unconscious until the cries of our daughter awakened me."

He touched the small form wonderingly, and Hayley knew he was not disappointed with a daughter but still she said, "I'm sorry I didn't produce a son."

"I'm not. I wanted a daughter just like you. We'll have a son the next time."

He closed his eyes, and Hayley looked anxiously at Nonna, who nodded encouragingly. Philip was bare to the waist, and a large bandage covered his chest. Apparently Nonna had saved his life, too. And looking around the building, Hayley noted some articles from their house—the Bible, her lute, and a few pieces of clothing. Nonna must have been busy in those few minutes after Hayley and Saponi had left the plantation.

Later in the day, carrying a string of fish she'd caught for their meal, Nonna ran into the barn and started flinging coverlets over Hayley and Philip.

Hayley gasped when a dirty cloth fell across her face, but Nonna pulled back the cover, and her black eyes conveyed a warning. She indicated that the baby's mouth should be covered and nodded toward the door.

"Opechancanough!"

Hayley had one quick glance into Philip's startled eyes before Nonna threw the blanket over her face again. Smothering under the rancid cloth, Hayley held her breath, praying the child wouldn't cry.

A faint guttural conversation could be heard outside the barn, but seemingly, the Indian chieftain didn't attempt to enter. When Hayley thought she would suffocate, Nonna drew back the covers.

"Gone!"

Nonna had protected them from her own father. But why? The answer was obvious to Hayley. Indian or English, women had the same capacity for loving. This woman's love for Philip had been greater than her hatred toward the English or her jealousy of Hayley.

Philip's eyes mirrored the relief Hayley felt. "She told Opechancanough she was waiting here until Saponi returned so they could come to the village."

"Saponi won't return, Philip." Hayley briefly related what had happened, not wanting to upset Philip in his weakened condition but realizing he should be told about his brother.

"Poor Mum," Philip murmured. "That is, if she still lives. I've been wondering all day what happened to her and Father."

"From what Saponi said, they are probably safe."

Under Nonna's care, both Philip and Hayley quickly regained their strength. How the girl ever procured enough food for them in that devastated region, Hayley never knew, but they always had something to eat—

198

perhaps nothing more than some bread made from ground acorns, or a roasted animal, or some broth, but the food nurtured their debilitated bodies.

Hayley was able to walk around before Philip was strong, and one afternoon when she moved to the door, two people were crossing the field, and she shuddered, thinking more natives were arriving.

"Philip, your parents are coming," she called excitedly when she recognized the pair. Running out of the barn, she called to them. "We're over here . . . safe."

When their tearful reunion was over, Hayley looked for Nonna to draw her into their rejoicing, for after all, she was family, too, but the Algonquian woman was gone. Seemingly, she had thought her responsibility was ended, and she had returned to her people.

Long into the night, the Lawrences discussed the terror of the past week.

"Jamestown suffered no damages at all. Right before we arrived, a Christian Indian boy, Chowan, told his master to alarm the settlers. And when we shared Saponi's warning with them, the people crowded into the fort, so the residents were prepared when the Indians attacked."

"But what about the rest of the colony? I saw many destroyed plantations when I walked along the James. And Saponi said it was a concentrated attack on the English."

Towaye shook his head, his face solemn. "News is bad. More than one-third of the English are dead. On some plantations, not one person is left. Even George Thorpe was killed, and his body badly abused."

"But why were they so cruel?" Hayley cried. "To kill women and children, and poor Mr. Thorpe, who was so good to them."

"Many Indian women and children have been killed by the settlers," Towaye explained. "The Algonquians thought this was their last chance to either destroy the English or be destroyed themselves. It was not treachery, as you might think, but the only way they knew to save *their* villages and families. It's a sad time for my people . . . a sad time for the colony."

"What happens now, Father?"

"The English will strike back. Already a ship has sailed for England with the news so that soldiers will be sent. The Algonquians are doomed."

"We're doomed, too, aren't we?" Hayley asked. "What can we do, Philip? Everything is gone, and with the colonists and the natives at war, what will happen to us?" She drew her baby close in her arms, already sensing the responsibility of protecting the child.

"We will start over again. When I began this plantation, I had only the earth and my two hands. Now I have you and the baby. Haywood will rise from the ashes; the Haywood of my dreams."

Maggie Lawrence and Towaye stayed with them until Philip gained enough strength to protect his family. Mistress Lawrence kissed them as she and Towaye prepared to go home.

"God has been good to us, my dear ones. He will see us through the trying times to come," she assured them. "He hasn't failed me yet."

Philip and Hayley watched until his parents disappeared into the greening forests; then they knelt beneath the oak tree where once before Philip had committed his future to the Lord. "As for me and my house, we will serve the Lord," he promised again. "The Lord gave, and the Lord hath taken away; blessed be the name of the Lord."

As Philip lifted Hayley to her feet and embraced her, a bluebird perched on a limb over their heads and pealed out a joyful song. Hayley laughed, assured that gentle spring had returned to Virginia, bringing a message of renewed hope.

ABOUT THE AUTHOR

A prolific author, IRENE BRAND has written two program books for women, a biography of a missionary, and three inspirational romances. In addition to books, Brand has published devotional literature, religious drama, and historical, general, and religious articles. *Come Gentle Spring,* a sequel to *Where Morning Dawns* (a recepient of the Award of Excellence at the Blue Ridge Christian Writers Conference, 1986), is her second romance for Serenade Books.

She teaches French and American history at a junior high school, and she is active in her local church. She lives with her husband, Rod, in West Virginia.

A Letter to Our Readers

Dear Reader:

Welcome to Serenade Books—a series designed to bring you beautiful love stories in the world of inspirational romance. They will uplift you, encourage you, and provide hours of wholesome entertainment, so thousands of readers have testified. That we might better contribute to your reading enjoyment, we would appreciate your taking a few minutes to respond to the following questions and return to:

> Lois Taylor
> Serenade Books
> The Zondervan Publishing House
> 1415 Lake Drive, S.E.
> Grand Rapids, Michigan   49506

1. Did you enjoy reading *Come Gentle Spring*?

   ☐ Very much. I would like to see more books by this author!
   ☐ Moderately
   ☐ I would have enjoyed it more if _____

2. Where did you purchase this book? _____

3. What influenced your decision to purchase this book?

   ☐ Cover   ☐ Back cover copy
   ☐ Title   ☐ Friends
   ☐ Publicity   ☐ Other _____

4. Please rate the following elements from 1 (poor) to 10 (superior).

☐ Heroine   ☐ Plot
☐ Hero   ☐ Inspirational theme
☐ Setting   ☐ Secondary characters

5. What are some inspirational themes you would like to see treated in future books?

_____

_____

6. Please indicate your age range:

☐ Under 18   ☐ 25–34   ☐ 46–55
☐ 18–24   ☐ 35–45   ☐ Over 55

Serenade / Saga books are inspirational romances in historical settings, designed to bring you a joyful, heart-lifting reading experience.

Serenade / Saga books available in your local bookstore:

#24 *To Dwell in the Land,* Elaine Watson
#25 *Moon for a Candle,* Maryn Langer
#26 *The Conviction of Charlotte Grey,*
    Jeanne Cheyney
#27 *Opal Fire,* Sandy Dengler
#28 *Divide the Joy,* Maryn Langer
#29 *Cimarron Sunset,* Peggy Darty
#30 *This Rolling Land,* Sandy Dengler
#31 *The Wind Along the River,* Jacquelyn Cook
#32 *Sycamore Settlement,* Suzanne Pierson Ellison
#33 *Where Morning Dawns,* Irene Brand
#34 *Elizabeth of Saginaw Bay,* Donna Winters
#35 *Westward My Love,* Elaine L. Schulte
#36 *Ransomed Bride,* Jane Peart
#37 *Dreams of Gold,* Elaine L. Schulte

Serenade/Saga books are now being published in a new, longer length:

#T1 *Chessie's King,* Kathleen Karr
#T2 *The Rogue's Daughter,* Molly Noble Bull
#T3 *Image in the Looking Glass,* Jacquelyn Cook
#T4 *Rising Thunder,* Carolyn Ann Wharton
#T5 *Fortune's Bride,* Jane Peart
#T6 *Cries the Wilderness Wind,* Susan Kirby